VOLUME THREE

EVERNIGHT PUBLISHING ®

www.evernightpublishing.com

MONSTERS OF NEW YORK

Copyright© 2025

ISBN: 978-0-3695-1289-5

Cover Artist: Jay Aheer

Editor: Lisa Petrocelli

VOLUME THREE

Monsters of New York is a sizzling paranormal romance series where passion collides with danger in the heart of the city that never sleeps. Each book introduces a new, irresistible shifter—each with its own dark secrets and primal desires. From wolves and bears to elusive creatures lurking in the shadows, these powerful beings navigate love, loyalty, and mystery in a world filled with human and supernatural monsters.

Set against the backdrop of New York's vibrant streets and hidden corners, every romance is an unforgettable journey where forbidden love and heated encounters could be the death of them—or the one thing that saves them. With danger always just around the corner, the shifters must face not only the threats of their own kind but the intense pull of a love that could change everything.

Uncover the secrets, feel the heat, and discover if love can tame the wildest beasts in Monsters of New York.

VOLUME THREE

WILDER OBSESSIONS

Monsters of New York

L.B. Martin

Copyright © 2025

"I can be changed by what happens to me. But I refuse to be reduced by it."
— Maya Angelou

VOLUME THREE

Prologue

Wilder

Three Years Ago

Never did I think I would be on this side of a gravestone, gazing down at the somber scene before me. This isn't how I envisioned my life unfolding. From the very first day of our union, I knew she wasn't my fated mate, but that didn't make me love her any less. I'm not even sure there is such a thing, as I've only heard stories passed down from the Elders. Never in my thirty-four years have I seen that kind of connection. The concept of a fated mate seems almost mythical, something passed down through generations like folklore. It is akin to the fairy tales humans grow up hearing.

My marriage to Emily was arranged to serve the interests of our father's business merger, and like the dutiful eldest son, I gave it my all. Everything was great until it wasn't. Now, here I stand in the freezing rain, watching as everyone in attendance opens their black umbrellas. Water ricochets in all directions, drenching my clothes, but I can't seem to care. The casket lowers to the ground and the gnawing pain in my chest intensifies until I'm doubled over, barely able to stand.

How did I get here?

****

Emily is sitting by the window, looking out at nothing in particular as her hand rests over her small belly. The sun dips behind the horizon, leaving a soft yet eerie glow that bathes the room in muted shadows. She didn't hear me approach, giving me a moment to see the toll this has taken on her. Soft tears slip down her cheeks, shattering my heart more than it already was.

"Em," I begin, but she doesn't turn. I take large strides across the room, needing to be closer to her. My heart hammers in my chest, each beat a reminder of the suffering festering between us. I see the dark circles underneath her lifeless eyes. There was a time when those amber orbs sparkled like molten gold under the sun, full of dreams and laughter. Now, they are hauntingly pale, dulled by despair.

I call her name again. "Em, you need to eat something." My voice is stern but soft. She still doesn't budge, forcing me to pull her chin up to see my face. Her once vibrant eyes remain vacant, as though she has locked herself away from the world. Something in her gaze ignites a deep-seated fear inside me, a primal instinct awakening within the depths of my being. Emily's skin is clammy and her warmth is no longer there.

"Emily," I demand, hating that I need to invoke my alpha's growl to reach her. But she doesn't even flinch, her body so tense it feels as though she exists in another realm. Panic rises, hot and fierce, clawing its way into my throat. I drop to my knees, pulling her limp body against mine. She leans into my arms, surrendering. In her weakened grasp is a small glass vial, hidden like a dagger. It slips from her hand and hits the floor, splintering into tiny shards, each piece reflected in my widening horror. A faint, mild scent wafts through the air, sweet yet sinister—the unmistakable aroma of nightshade, a toxic poison that twists my gut into knots. My heart hammers faster, adrenaline surging through my veins as I rise, clutching Emily's small frame against my chest and laying her gently on our bed.

"Emily." I shake her lightly, desperation coating my voice. "Wake up! Please." But there's no response. Nothing. My breathing turns erratic as I look down at

her. The chilling truth hits me like a freight train. This isn't her fault. The pregnancy had been brutal, both physically and emotionally, and we have both been drowning in our own grief. I was too consumed by my own devastation to notice the silent anguish ripping Emily apart. How could I be so blind? Why didn't I see the signs?

"Emily," I plead, stroking the brown hair from her face. "Dammit! Why did you do this to me? To us?" I shout, my voice breaking as anger courses through me. I pull out my phone, my fingers trembling as I navigate the screen.

"I need you here now! Emily—" I croak out, choking on the words. "She drank nightshade. Bring every antidote you have, James!" I throw my phone onto the bed, the dread pooling in my stomach matching the growing knot in my throat. Emily lies lifelessly as my hand shakes over hers. Logically, I know there's no way to reverse what she's done, but I'll be damned if I sit by idly as her life fades away. I pull her body to mine, cradling her against my chest and praying to the gods. Please, let her live.

Time stretches endlessly, every second feeling like an eternity before I hear heavy footsteps storming up the stairs. I hold my breath, willing it not to be too late. James bursts through the door, a wildfire of urgency igniting in his dark eyes.

"Wilder!" He takes in the scene with one sweeping glance, and I know he sees the desperation etched across my face. He runs his hands through his hair, letting out a heavy sigh as he digs through his bag, retrieving a syringe filled with a glowing blue antidote.

"This won't—" he begins but I cut him off.

"Don't! Just do it!" I lay Emily back down on the bed. My heart sinks further into despair as I watch his

face fall the moment his gaze lands on my wife. Her lips are blue and her skin is even paler than before. My brain understands that it's too late but my heart is what's demanding James to bring her back. To bring my wife back to me.

James injects the antidote into Emily's arm, the seconds dripping away like thick molasses. But when no sign of life comes, his shoulders sag, and hopelessness sweeps over him.

"It's too late," he murmurs.

A roar erupts from my puma, echoing like thunder through the confines of my soul, shattering the calm of my heart and the fragile peace within me. I can't hold him back, this devastation ignites something fierce and primal. I have to escape.

In a wild flurry, my clothes tear as my powerful beast emerges, breaking free from the shackles of grief. I run, my form a blur of black fur against the white backdrop of snow, racing through the forest, each step a desperate attempt to flee from the haunting reality.

Emily is dead.

My wife. My mate. Gone.

The agony is ripping me apart and I can't fucking breathe.

Snowflakes thickly blanket the ground, each one whispering her name. I howl at the moon, the pain ripping through me like frayed barbs of reality. My vision blurs as my puma breaks through the boundary of our home into the endless wilderness, and I'm swallowed by the woods.

Hours blend into one another, time morphs into a relentless beast of its own making. When my muscles finally give out, I collapse into the crisp, frozen earth, lying on my side like a withering flower, suffocating under the weight of despair.

This is what heartbreak must feel like—a slow, bitter demise of hope, unforgiving and cruel.

I howl again, raw and untamed, my voice echoing through the haunting silence of the ever-stirring forest. The sound is a wild, tortured cry, a primal confession of loss and pain, yet it feels futile. Each note of anguish only deepens the scars. I know it will never leave me. Eventually, the forest quiets, and with resolve, I shift back to human form, the bitter cold biting at my bare flesh. I drag myself back, stepping into the darkness that awaits, knowing my life will never be the same. A part of me died tonight, right along with Emily, and I can feel that void gaping inside me.

My feet carry me along the icy trails, hoping not to encounter any wandering animals. Even if I were to come across a wolf or a coyote, it could be an interesting challenge to take my mind off what the fuck is waiting for me when I walk through the doors to my house.

We're the largest and most lethal shifter clan on this side of the mountain range, but no matter how strong and ruthless a person appears, their heart is never impervious from the inevitable breakdown of being vulnerable. When that person isn't human, but a shifter who's lost everything, they're not just vulnerable but also become something darker—a wrathful storm brewed from the ashes of love and despair. And that's what I'm about to become—dangerous.

Tonight, I am reborn from heartbreak's ashes, birthed anew like a terrible phoenix ready to unleash hell upon a world that has stolen my brightest light. Their cries, the pain of their lost souls, will be my anthem, for I am a shifter—transformed by love, transfigured by loss.

Danger will become my essence, and in the dark, I will dance with sorrow, powerful, relentless, and alive.

****

As my mind returns to the present, I realize the ceremony ended and I've been left alone at her graveside. The rain weeps from the heavens, a torrent of grief that mirrors the tumult within my heart. I stand staring off at the mountains of Colorado, their once-majestic peaks now shrouded in clouds, a gray pallor that steals the vibrance from the landscape.

It no longer feels like home.

The storm of rage and grief within me is relentless, a tempest that threatens to consume everything in its path. Every step I take away from her grave feels heavier, as if the very ground is pulling me back, demanding I face the torment that gnaws at my soul.

The rain continues to pour, soaking through my clothes and seeping into my bones, but I barely feel it. My thoughts are a chaotic swirl of memories and pain, interspersed with flashes of uncontrollable anger. I clench my fists, feeling my nails bite into my palms, grounding me just enough to keep moving.

My mind drifts and I question everything, perhaps that's what devastation does to you. It eats at your soul until there's nothing left but a shell of the person you once were. In the corners of my memory, I can still hear her laughter, the tinkling sound like wind chimes dancing in the summer air, but now it feels miles away—a ghost echoing within the caverns of my shattered heart.

Hope is a distant, fragile thing, nearly suffocated by the searing rage that consumes me. The loss of my wife has awakened something dark within me, a fury that claws at my insides, demanding an outlet. My muscles ache not from grief alone, but from the sheer effort of keeping my puma at bay. He's restless, dangerous, and I feel his anger coursing through my veins.

"I just hope my rage won't be the end of me," I mutter under my breath, a bitter acknowledgment of the darkness festering inside. I've seen what unchecked fury can do—it destroys lives, ruins relationships, leaving nothing but ashes in its wake. Yet here I am, teetering on the edge, my puma restless and dangerous, pushing me toward a path I might not return from.

I need to get away, to find some semblance of peace before my anger consumes me whole. The mountains of Colorado, once a place of solace and familiarity, now feel like a prison, their towering peaks casting long, dark shadows over my life. I can no longer find comfort in their embrace, instead, they mock my pain, a constant reminder of everything I've lost.

As I begin my journey into the unknown, I can only hope that somewhere along the way, I find a means to tame the beast within. To channel my rage into something other than destruction. Because if I don't, I fear there will be nothing left of the man I once was.

VOLUME THREE

Chapter One

Wilder

Present Time

New York City bustles with an electric energy that has my insides fighting to be released. Why I ever thought I could live in a city and coexist with humans is beyond me. My patience is tested every day, leaving me feral. The bell over the door chimes, making me grit my teeth. If I have to deal with another dumb fuck today, I can't be held accountable for my actions.

"Wilder, my man!" Kody booms from behind the counter. At least it's not a human. He found me when I first moved to the city and introduced me to an underground shifter fight club below the exclusive bar, The Gin Room. Shifters can seek out other like-minded individuals so I instantly knew he wasn't human. Being a dragon shifter, he knows the difficulties in keeping a lid on his aggression, hence the illegal fighting scene.

"Haven't seen you around in a while," I mention, throwing back a glass of whiskey. It's basically closing time and with the day I've had, I needed something to take the edge off.

"Yeah," he trails off, looking around my custom motorcycle shop. I've got a few beauties on display for when my high-end customers come in. "You've been busy?"

"Something like that. People don't realize a custom motorcycle builder's job isn't just tuning engines. I have a waiting list longer than the line at Halley's." I lean back against the bar, tapping my fingers in an anxious rhythm.

"Well, Black Thunder Motorcycles is the best in the state. Fuck, maybe the country. You need to hire more employees so you aren't working your life away."

"I don't like people. You know this," I remind him.

Kody chuckles, shaking his head. "You need to let go of that tension, man. By the way, there's a fight tonight. Want in?"

That piques my interest. It's been a while since I was in the ring, slamming my claws into some unsuspecting soul. The adrenaline rush soothes the anger buried deep within, if only for a little while.

"Who's the opponent?" I ask, not that it really matters. I could kill any motherfucker who crosses me. It doesn't always get that far, depending on whether the fight is to the death, and most of mine are. *Why the hell would I waste my time on some pansy tap-out session if I can kill the beast?*

"Draken," he answers, making me snap my head to his. My brow furrows, and I can't help but laugh.

"Does he have a death wish?"

"Apparently. He's been running his mouth that he can beat your ass." Kody raises an eyebrow, a sly grin forming on his lips. "He's gotten the attention of the club bidders."

That makes me bark out a laugh. Draken is a coyote shifter and a fool if he thinks his skills could ever compare to mine. "That little mutt thinks he can take me? He's more delusional than I thought!"

"Hey, don't sleep on the guy. He's got speed, just be careful," Kody warns as he helps himself to my liquor, then leans against the desk.

"Speed? Fuck, he'll be greasing up the floor before I even break a sweat," I remark, refilling my glass and feeling the spark of competition ignite inside me.

"Just remember, it's not just about you out there." Kody grins, lifting his glass in my direction. "You have a reputation to uphold."

I nudge him with my shoulder. "Yeah, yeah. I know. I'm the wild card," I smirk, but beneath it lies raw anticipation.

The city hums across all the walls of my shop, the night serenading the hidden beasts that walk among humans. I finish my drink and catch Kody's eye. "When do I have to be there?"

"Midnight at The Gin Room." He raises his glass, and I join him with my own half-full tumbler. "You're going to smash his face so hard he'll think he's fighting a fucking freight train."

"Always the best hype man," I add, clapping him on the back. My mood lifts as the thrill of the fight floods my veins. Kody is the only one in this city who knows about my past. He knew I was escaping something dark when he found me on the streets that first week I got here. I was a mess, slumming it in the alleys, taking anything as long as it took the pain away for a couple hours. As much as I tried to push him away, he kept coming around, until he finally grew on me. I got cleaned up and started my own business, and I have to say, the money is top notch. He's the only friend I have since leaving my old life in Colorado behind.

"Brothers, man," he corrects, slinging the rest of his bourbon back.

The clock strikes twelve as we walk into The Gin Room, a rich upscale bar in the heart of the city. This place is known for its exclusivity, meaning only the wealthy can pass through those doors. Fortunately, my business affords me such luxuries. The first floor opens to a large, lavish bar tucked between private velvety, leather booths. Black marble covers every surface, making it gleam under the twinkling lights above. All of the handcrafted cocktails are served by well-dressed bartenders as the patrons mingle. A low thrum of music whisks through the room, sending a few couples to the dance floor. The atmosphere is sophisticated without being suffocating. This isn't a bar I frequent for drinks, but when I do, the opulence is always impressive.

Instead of taking a right into the main floor, Kody and I make our way down a long corridor, then down the spiral staircase to the lower level. The dim lights strain to illuminate the throng of eager faces crowding the underground arena. The scent of sweat mixed with liquor and primal energy fills my nostrils. The roars of the crowd, a cacophony urging me to unleash chaos. I can feel my beast stirring, clawing at the human side of me, pushing for release. *We needed this.*

"Wilder, you made it!" a familiar voice calls out, and I spot Lena, a wolf shifter with a fierce reputation of her own. "You're not backing out, are you?" She steps closer, her eyes sparkling with mischief. She's a drunken mistake from a year ago, but that doesn't stop her from pawing at me every chance she gets.

"I don't back out of challenges. Now, where is this little coyote wannabe?" I smile, looking through the crowd for my next victim.

"He's in the back, throwing a fit. He didn't expect you to take up the offer. You rattled him more than you know," she explains, her voice laced with excitement. Kody throws his head back in a laugh.

"Well, my boy needed to unleash some aggression," he says and smirks. Lena's eyes flare, thinking he means something more than a fight. *Not fucking happening.*

"Just the fight," I add, directed at her, causing Kody to bark out another laugh.

"Come on, let's get you checked in." I nod, following him to the back of the room. We pass the ring where two wolves are fighting with no finesse.

"You know you could have your pick of anyone in here. Why not take Lena up on her offer? She's dying for another sample of Wilder Black," he hollers above the crowd.

"I don't double dip. You know that."

"Of course I do. Every chick in here knows. But that doesn't make them any less determined to be the one to tame your beast." He laughs, making me roll my eyes. He can joke all he wants but he knows I will never go down that road again. It's not in my genes anymore.

"Black, it's about time I see you around here again," the older gentleman behind the table announces, making several people turn in my direction. My reputation precedes me everywhere I go.

"Well, you can thank Kody." I slap him on the back, making him cough. We may be close to the same height but he doesn't refine his power like I do. Day after day, I retreat to my home gym, where I beat the shit out of the dummies I had specially made. They are on a constant shipping schedule to my penthouse because of how fast I tear through them.

"You're up after one of those kids gets knocked out." He gestures to the two behind us.

"They seem to be getting younger and younger," I muse.

"Well, they all want to beat the notorious Black." He chuckles, throwing me a towel.

"There's only room for one of us." I wink, turning on my heels to the changing rooms.

"You're incorrigible," Kody jokes, shooting me a look.

"As advertised," I taunt.

"For fuck's sake. Why does my friend have to be a lunatic?"

"You're the one that wouldn't leave me alone, if I remember correctly?" I laugh.

Kody rolls his eyes. "Going to grab a drink. Your usual?" I nod as he leaves me to change into my shorts, so I don't tear through my suit.

My human tailor is already terrified of me. If she wasn't the number-one around, I would find someone new. Unfortunately, she's the best of the best, but I don't think she appreciates it when I bring her the scraps of designer suits I've destroyed. I chuckle, thinking of her horrified expression the last time I met with her. Poor little thing genuinely didn't know I was a shifter and I've never seen someone as pale as her in my life.

The crowd hushes as the announcer calls my name, "Wilder Black is in the house tonight!" Cheers boom around me and my heart races with palpable energy. I step into the ring, the spotlight pouring down on me, and in the opposite corner, Draken stands, a cocky grin plastered on his face. The fucker doesn't truly believe he signed his death sentence.

I feel alive, electric energy coursing through me as the crowd surges with fervor. They are the shifters—creatures who bear the likeness of their animal kin, and tonight they cheer for both blood and glory. The weight of their eyes presses down on my shoulders, igniting a fire within me that demands to be unchained.

"What's up, Wilder? Finally decided to join the big leagues?" he taunts, flexing as he prances around the ring. Dumb coyote thinks he's cool shit when in reality he's about to be no better than roadkill.

"Sure, if the big leagues mean hand-delivering your wildly unfounded ass-whooping, then absolutely," I retort, rolling my shoulders as I prepare for combat. A flicker of fear flashes through his eyes but he schools his features quickly.

"Surrender, pup." I taunt, basking in the cheers around me. "Then maybe I'll make your death quick."

"Enough talk!" the announcer bellows toward us. Then he pulls the microphone back to his mouth. "The rules of tonight's fight are as follows: tap-outs aren't allowed. This is a fight to the death in shifter form." The audience cheers, the noise almost deafening. They don't get this kind of fight all the time. Tap-outs are the usual around here but that's not my style.

"Black, Sonner, shift!" he roars over the speakers. Immediately, my muscles tense, rippling beneath my skin as I feel the change coming. It starts deep within, a primal call I can no longer resist. My breath quickens, eyes flickering from human to intense, inky black as my vision sharpens. My bones begin to shift, elongating and realigning with a series of cracks that echo around me. I bite back a growl, pain giving way to raw power. My skin darkens, sprouting sleek, midnight fur that shimmers under the dim lights. Each heartbeat pounds louder, a drumbeat in sync with the earth's pulse. As my fingers retract into formidable claws, my face elongates into a proud, fierce muzzle. With a final, guttural snarl, my transition is complete.

Standing there on all fours, I wait for my opponent's shift completion as raw, untamed power flows through me. My senses are heightened, every sound, scent, and movement acutely clear to me. Draken stands in his coyote form, his amber eyes gleaming with cunning and malice.

My puma's spirit surges forward, needing blood. The boundaries blur, it's not just a fight—it's a liberation. I'm a ruthless killer and only a deranged fighter would dare get in the ring with me. That's why my fights have become far and few between. I'm undefeated and tonight won't be any different. It's a pity I don't have more adversaries, forcing my beast to remain shackled most of the time.

"Fight!" the announcer shouts. We circle each other, my muscles coiled and ready to fight. Draken's lips curl back in a snarl, revealing sharp fangs as he lunges forward, and like an electrical current coursing through my body, I charge like I'm on a speeding motorcycle.

He's swift, darting around like the coyote he is, but every glance I take sears an image of his form in my mind's eye. I won't let him evade my blows for long.

Our bodies collide with a force that sends reverberations through the ground beneath us. My claws rake across Draken's flank, leaving deep gashes that begin oozing blood. He howls in pain but quickly recovers, snapping his jaw at my hind leg. He manages to clamp down but I twist my body, dislodging the coyote and retaliating with a swipe of my paw that sends Draken sprawling.

Each jab, each dodge sharpens my senses, a dance of fluid aggression. I can feel the eyes of the crowd, the shifters living vicariously through our bout.

Panting heavily, he scrambles to his feet, his eyes narrowing as he calculates his next move. Stupid coyote feints to the left, then darts to the right trying to get my vulnerable underbelly. But I already anticipated his move, leaping over Draken with a grace that belies my size. I land behind him, sinking my teeth into his shoulder and shaking him violently.

Draken yelps, writhing under my grasp. Desperation lends him strength and he manages to twist free, delivering a vicious bite to my ear. I roar in pain as my blood splatters to the ground. Now we are locked in a deadly dance, our growls and snarls echoing through the room.

With a final powerful swipe, I knock Draken off his feet, making him land hard. He's dazed and disoriented which I use to my advantage as I pounce on my fallen opponent, pinning him to the ground. My jaws close around Draken's throat, a low growl rumbling from deep within my chest.

Draken's struggles grow weaker until he finally lays still, defeated. I release my grip, standing over my vanquished foe. The sound of my ragged breathing fills my ears until the crowd erupts into a frenzy of chaos. People are yelling about bets won and some small fights break out over salty losers.

"The Notorious Black is still undefeated!" the announcer yells through the intercom, making my beast roar. I feel the familiar searing heat spreading through my body, signaling the change back to my human form. Every muscle screams in protest as my bones begin to contract and shift, the powerful form of the puma giving way to my human shape. The sleek black fur retracts, leaving me bare. My vision blurs, transitioning from the sharp, predatory clarity to the more familiar, less acute human sight. The pain is excruciating but familiar, an inevitable part of my dual nature. My chest heaves and my limbs tremble with exhaustion, but the adrenaline of the win flows through my blood.

I throw my fists up in victory, my body radiating the high of battle. I'm intoxicated by the aftermath of the fight, the way the euphoria wraps around me like a warm embrace.

"Anyone else think they can take me?" I growl, causing a visible shudder through the crowd. Not a damn person steps up—*pity*. This fight didn't last nearly long enough for my liking.

As the medics remove the mangled animal, I

allow myself these moments of calm that envelop my inner puma. It is a reminder that within this chaotic city, I can still unleash my true self—an instinctual creature thriving on emotion, power, and the primal need for freedom.

Kody tosses me a towel and my shorts, pulling me through the crowd of everyone chanting my name.

"*Black*!"

"*Black*!"

"*Black*!"

I wipe the sweat from my face and chest, seeing the blood stain the towel. Fortunately, I heal quickly but I hate that the motherfucker drew my own blood. I need more fights before I lose my reputation.

"Thanks to you, I raked in 100K." He smiles, making me roll my eyes.

"Did you doubt my abilities?"

"Fuck, no! My boy always pulls out a win! Let's go celebrate," he suggests. "We can go upstairs after you shower." He holds his nose as if this whole damn place doesn't smell like a fucking farm.

"I'll shower, but I don't feel like being around rich bastards like you tonight." I laugh at his appalled face.

"You're richer than me, Black!"

"Yep, and don't forget it. Now, go find your usual harem." I roll my eyes. "I'm going to find somewhere new to go," I reply as I duck into the shower.

"One of these days I'll convince you how good it can be with multiple women at your disposal," he shouts over the sound of the pelting water on my skin.

"I don't need lots of women to convince me that I have a huge dick like you do, brother." I laugh. I hear his irritated huff as he leaves me in peace. *Fucking finally*. I love the guy but I like my alone time. I don't need someone to fill the quiet in my life.

VOLUME THREE

Chapter Two

Arwen

Being a bartender at Alley Katz isn't the worst job in the world. Yes, I wish I could work someplace where my ass isn't slapped and groped every night, but at least I make good tips—something I desperately need right now.

I pull on my signature red-and-black lace corset, tightening the ribbons on the back myself. The fabric clinches my waist, a gentle reminder of the curves that draw wandering eyes. I zip the bottom so it hugs me nicely, gliding over my hips and accentuating their thickness, a trait that has become both a blessing and a curse.

With each flick of my brush, I paint stories upon my skin: tales of seduction and survival, masked beneath silky silver hair that cascades down in loose waves. I've always had this unusual colored hair, which most people think I've dyed myself. I was born with this lustrous silver that almost seems to sparkle at times.

I give myself a once-over in the mirror, ensuring my makeup is flawless—smoky eyes and bold red lipstick, a look that commands attention like a song begging to be heard. My chest tightens as I look at myself, not recognizing the woman I've become. *How did I get here?* I had dreams. I wanted to make something of myself, but here I am fighting for my life every day.

Jarrod wasn't always like this. When we first met in college, he swept me off my feet with his good looks and charm. His smoldering brown eyes and toned body lured me into his trap. *But all good things come to an end, right?* It's like a switch was flipped in him when we moved in together. He forced me to quit school to get a job to pay for everything. Meanwhile, he began wasting away on drugs and alcohol. He lost his medical scholarship, which he blames me for and began taking out his anger on me. The truth was, he got in with the wrong crowd of people at school and that's when his drug use started. Nevertheless, I'm his personal punching bag when something doesn't go his way. The first time it happened, he dropped to his knees before me and cried for hitting me, begging me for forgiveness. My heart broke for him so I tried to get him help.

He went to a doctor one time and was diagnosed with "intermittent explosive behavior." The diagnosis angered him so badly, he threw the psychiatrist's desk across the room, freaking her out. He ended up threatening to kill her if she ever told anyone what happened and I guess she didn't because no police ever came to take him away like I hoped they would.

That's when things went from bad to worse. Now here I am years later, looking at the shell of the girl I once was. Determined to proceed with my plan, I straighten my shoulders and remind myself I won't die here. I *will* get out and I *will* finally have peace.

Taking a deep breath, I slip on my high-heeled, knee-high boots, then turn in the mirror to make sure everything is in place, mentally preparing for the chaos of the night ahead. The music, the crowd, the endless orders for drinks, can be overwhelming. I lean into the mirror to ensure the bruises have been covered well enough, not allowing a single hint of the reality I face each night to seep into the professional façade I have created.

After all, I don't need more questions than I already get from Kit, my boss and reluctant confidante. She watches me like a hawk before every shift, and though she never openly asks, I can see the concern in her sharp blue eyes. I remember the night I stumbled into

Alley Katz, fresh from a bruising incident that left me shaken, and how she offered me a job with a glimmer of empathy. I feel her understanding from the way her gaze softens each time I don my work attire. I often wonder how she knows what nightmares I return home to every night. It's like she can read my mind, or maybe I'm just not good at hiding it.

Grabbing my bag, I head toward the door as my boyfriend calls out behind me. The sound of his voice slithers through the air, grating against my skin.

"Well, don't you look like a fat whore. It's a wonder you make any tips at all," he sneers as he saunters over to me. Shivers crawl down my spine. I was hoping I could slip out tonight without him noticing since he'd been so drunk this afternoon, making him pass out.

"You know this is the usual uniform for the bar. We need the money, Jarrod. Just let me—"

His laughter cuts through my voice like a serrated knife. "Yeah, well, I wouldn't appreciate being waited on by your fat ass." He grabs my hips hard, no doubt leaving more marks behind. I wince from the pain, turning my face so he doesn't see. It will only land me in more trouble.

"Too bad I never made it to medical school. I could slice you up until you were my perfect little doll," he chuckles darkly. Bile rises in my throat, knowing he still would use his precious knife on me, degree or not. His proclivity to use the blade on me increases by the day. He makes a slicing noise as his fingers trail over me, as though he's cutting away all my imperfections. I barely eat as it is because there's no money left after he gets his hands on it. At the thought of food, my stomach grumbles.

"See, you're always hungry. This is why I limit your food intake or you'd be as big as a house." He holds his arms out wide, showing me how large I would be.

"Anyways, make sure you earn enough tonight for me to get my weed and pills tomorrow. It's the only way I can stand the sight of you."

"Then why don't you let me go?" I murmur, wishing my voice was stronger. A tear falls to my cheek and without warning, Jarrod's hand is flying through the air slapping my face. A gasp of pain bubbles out of my mouth, causing his eyes to darken.

"Oh, my little Arwen, you'll never be free of me. Your holes are still tight and you bring me money, so you're still of use," he muses. "Maybe you need to get on your knees right now and show me how thankful you are to have a man put up with your shit." My breath gets choked in my throat as he presses his hands down on my shoulders.

"J-Jarrod, I'm going to be late—"

I want to yell, to scream that I deserve more than his scorn and disdain, but a lump forms in my throat. In the fleeting silence, I can feel the heat of anger rising, an inferno threatening to engulf my nerves. But I know better, so I grind my teeth instead, swallowing my pride.

"Hmm, saved by the clock I suppose, but be ready to take it in your throat and ass as soon as you get home, my little cum-dumpster." He roughly slams his fingers into my mouth then pulls me forward.

"I can see that look in your eyes. Don't ever think I won't own you in every way, so you better keep coming up with good excuses for those marks. If I go down, I'm taking you with me." His threat lingers in the air, forcing me to change the subject or he'll never let me leave.

"I'll get you your money," I reassure with a forced smile, hoping it looks natural. I just need a little more cash before I can start over in a new city with a new name. Somewhere he can't find me. I think of the stash I hid behind a loose brick in my closet. I am so close to freedom I can taste it. The desperation to escape his harm fuels every step I take.

His anger is palpable, affecting the very air around us. He wraps his fingers around my throat, pushing me against the rough wooden door. My heart races, pounding like war drums in my chest.

"You better not be lying to me," he growls, his voice vibrating with menace. I can feel the heat of his slimy breath against my skin. "I don't want to hear any excuses this time. If you don't bring home enough, you'll regret it. You know what happens when you disappoint me." Undeniable fear wraps around my chest, making it hard to breathe.

"I'll get it, I promise," I wheeze, stars starting to dance in my eyes from the lack of oxygen. My heart races, and I can feel a cold sweat forming on my back. The fear of his wrath is a constant shadow, and I know I have to get away from him before it's too late.

He shoves me up against the wall and drops his arms, scoffing as he turns away. I swallow, trying to alleviate the pain, and hurry to leave, my head pounding and my breathing shallow. As soon as the front door is locked behind me, tears fall freely down my face. A mix of relief and pure rage churns in my gut. I wish I had a family to turn to but of course I was an orphan. My parents didn't want me and neither did any of the foster homes. The only thing that got me through the hurt was to lose myself in songs. Singing has always been my passion, almost like it's ingrained in my very soul. Jarrod can't stand the sound of it and forbids me to sing at home. He's always saying it makes him feel weird. I don't understand why my voice affects him so much. It's always been a mystery.

The night air feels like a lifeline, and I gulp it in,

trying to steady my racing heart. I have to get through tonight. Just a little more money, and I'll be free. His words feel like poison, wrapping around my heart. *"You'll never be free of me."* They echo in my ears like the tolling of a death knell, and the burning resolve within me grows like a flame fueled by pure terror. The bar might not be perfect, but it's my escape from him, even if just for a few hours.

As I approach the entrance, the familiar hum of music and chatter grows louder. I slip through the back entrance and greet the bouncer, Jim, as he checks his clipboard and opens the metal door.

"Evening, Arwen. You ready for another late night?"

"Always," I reply, forcing a smile. Scanning the space, I see the two bartenders that worked the day shift, hustling through the sea of people. This place can get really busy during the weekend and tonight is no exception.

The usual crowd is already here, filling the space with laughter, conversation, and the clinking of glasses. I make my way behind the bar, slipping into my role as if putting on a mask. The night starts like any other, with the usual rush of orders and the comforting rhythm of work. Leaning down behind the counter, goose bumps erupt over my skin when I hear a low, raspy voice in front of me asking for a drink.

"Whiskey, neat," he orders in a deep, commanding voice that sends shivers down my spine. I look up to see the most vibrant and alluring yellow eyes I've ever seen. The older man is huge, even seated, I know he's probably a foot taller than me. Something crosses his handsome face when I stand and reach for the bottle behind the bar. My hands tremble slightly as I pour the amber liquid into a glass, my thoughts racing.

"Coming right up," I stammer, trying to sound casual despite the storm brewing inside me. *Why is he looking at me like that?* I feel like prey caught in a predator's trap.

He watches me intently, his gaze unwavering, as if I'm the only thing of interest in his world. I can feel heat creeping up my neck, a blush I can't control. He's the most striking man I've ever encountered. His shoulder-length black hair frames a chiseled face, and the tattoos snaking down his arms only enhance his intimidating yet captivating presence. He's definitely older than me but I don't know by how much. He doesn't have a single gray hair but there's a dark wisdom that seems to radiate from him.

"Thanks," he says, his voice smooth yet powerful, pulling me even deeper into this strange connection. He gulps it in one sip, his lips pressing against the rim of the glass, and my heart races as our fingers brush together when I retrieve the glass from the bar. Fire blossoms through my whole body at the brief contact, and I try my best to keep my cool. *Holy shit, why do I feel this way?* I've touched hundreds of patrons, and never have I reacted like this.

"I've never seen you here before," he muses.

As I pull my hand back slowly, I gasp when he wraps his fingers around it, sealing me in a bond I never anticipated. Every inch of me is alight, and I know I should pull away, but it feels like my body has a mind of its own, entranced by the warm callouses of his skin caressing the back of my hand.

"I've been working here for a while," I manage to squeak out, desperately trying to remain professional and push away the burning tingle his touch ignites within me. "Guess our paths just haven't crossed."

He smiles—a slow, almost predacious grin that

makes my heart skip a beat. "What's your name?" he asks, leaning forward slightly, drawing me deeper into his magnetic pull. "It's not every day I meet someone as intriguing as you … Starlight." His words flow over me like warm honey, wrapping around my senses and affecting me unlike anything I've ever felt.

"My name is Arwen," I reply, the syllables barely escaping my lips as our eyes lock, the warmth swirling between us intoxicating.

He chuckles, the sound low and rumbling, sending a shiver through me. "Arwen. A name as beautiful as the stars you're likened to."

We stare at each other for a moment, before a voice beside us clears its throat. Kit is standing there, staring at me, an eyebrow raised in question. My face heats, and I duck behind the bar, retrieving a beer from the cooler. I can feel Kit's eyes on me and my ears grow hot with embarrassment. *Why is it that every time I look at this guy, my stomach ties itself into a million knots?*

The mysterious man begins to look me over with his heated gaze. Soon, anger flashes in his eyes, causing me to step away, instinctively covering my throat, somehow knowing he can see the marks left from my past. The scars are my enemies, dark reminders of the shackles I wear.

After a few seconds of tense silence, I walk away to help the rest of the people waiting for drinks. I glance back, catching him with a woman hanging all over him, probably ready to buy him the expensive champagne I bet he's used to. That is if her assets aren't blocking the bottle. I chuckle to myself, trying to mask my feelings with humor. But with every step I take, I'm left wondering where the fire that blazed so furiously earlier had suddenly extinguished, leaving him stone cold.

Suddenly, the man's voice cuts through the noise

of the bar, "What happened to you?" His tone is rife with concern and a controlled fury that surprises me. "Who did this?"

Tears prick my eyes at his bluntness. I hate being seen as this pathetic human, trapped in an abusive relationship I haven't found the courage to escape. I try to formulate a reasonable explanation, one that won't lead to him demanding to know the source of my scars. But before a single thought can solidify, the first tear falls.

His eyes soften as he sees the truth etched on my face. The weight of his gaze feels unbearable, and I know it's too late—I've bared my soul beneath the harsh lights of this clandestine bar. I begin wiping tears off my cheeks as an internal battle plays out behind his hard exterior I sense his restraint, like a coiled spring ready to snap.

"I'm sorry. It's time for my break," I stammer, the vulnerability in my voice sharper than I intended. Without waiting for a response, I rush through the back, barreling through the exit. Kit is still managing the bar and will cover for me for a few minutes while I try to compose myself.

Outside, the cool night air kisses my flushed cheeks, and I lean against the wall, desperately trying to catch my breath. Lyrics pop in my head, so I close my eyes and begin to sing to myself. The vibrations of my voice circle around me, pulling me from my despair and lifting my heart. My song washes over me like a wave, calming my mind and body, providing a rare moment of peace against the constant turmoil. Singing has always seemed meditative to me and I guess that's one positive thing I can hold onto. I hear footsteps beside me and hesitate to glance over, fearing what I might see. My song stops, bringing back the agony. Crying isn't an option. I can't allow anyone to see me at a moment of weakness. Jarrod hates when I cry. He won't let me explain my emotions, it only makes him angrier when I do. So, I've learned to hide my feelings. Now I'm out behind the building in a dirty alleyway, alone and shaking. I'm disgusted with the level of despair I've allowed myself to fall to in his presence.

"Arwen!" The voice rings out, that same low rumble that floods my mind with thoughts of warmth and danger. "Wait!"

I turn, caught in a moment of hesitation, and there he stands—my mysterious stranger, now devoid of that entertaining woman, his eyes searching for mine.

A sob erupts from my throat. *Fuck. Why does this always happen to me? Why is everything falling apart, like this world is determined to kick me while I'm down?*

"You can't just walk away like that," he demands, frustration and concern intermingling. "Who hurt you?"

I lock eyes with him, searching for an escape, but I feel the gravity of his presence firmly anchoring me. He gently wraps his arms around me and pulls me against him. To my surprise, his touch is reassuring, the gentle caress of his fingers sending a rush of relief and security through me.

"What's your name?" I whisper, my voice barely escaping me.

"Wilder," he says softly, contrasting the storm inside me with his calmness.

With each exhale, the stress of the day escapes my lungs until I have nothing left. I lift my face to meet his eyes, only now noticing how close we're standing, our breaths mingling. An understanding settles over him as his eyes narrow, searching for an answer that my body has betrayed. My cheeks flame, and I want to pull away from his closeness.

"Who did this to you?" he repeats, trailing his fingers over my neck, causing me to involuntarily flinch.

Anger flashes in his eyes, but I know it's not directed at me.

My heart is racing as he stares me down and I shiver as his anger becomes palpable. The black pupils constrict and dilate, betraying his intense emotions. He leans back and closes his eyes for a second, then he exhales, shakes his head, and glances to the side. When he looks at me, his eyes have returned to their natural light-yellow hue.

He swallows hard, as if coming to a decision, then leans back to look at me, eyes unblinking.

"It's nothing," I lie, trying to put distance between us.

"Don't fucking lie to me," he demands. "How long?"

"Why do you care?" I fire back, taking another step away. His presence makes my head spin, like I can't get enough of it, like he has an addicting draw that I didn't know existed. He gives me an irritated expression, and my eyes widen when the gold in his irises seem to change color and darken slightly. *Is that normal?*

"Tell me." His face holds a blank expression, but his tone is dark with a threat.

"Only a couple years..." My gaze lowers, hoping he'll be satisfied and move on. My mind is playing tug-of-war as the pain rushes back, and Wilder's reaction intensifies.

"I'll kill him!" he shouts, startling me. His fists are tight, veins popping. He seems to want to keep me safe. But no, I have to maintain distance.

Why is he so angry? Why does it seem like he wants to help me?

"No. It's my fault." I lower my eyes to the ground again, trying to take a deep breath. Jarrod always convinces me that my circumstances are because I'm not good enough. I'm too fat, and I don't make enough money to support all of his habits.

Tears threaten the corners of my eyes. I'm terrified of what Wilder will do now that he knows my situation. *Will he go after Jarrod?*

Wilder may be bigger than Jarrod, but I don't need someone fighting my battles. I'm so close to getting out from under Jarrod. I only need a couple hundred dollars for the bus ticket and enough money to live on until I find a new job.

"You better start talking, and tell me what happened, right fucking now," he seethes, grabbing my arms. He pulls me in closer and lowers his voice. He's careful with his tone, but his hold is like a vice. "Arwen, you won't like how this will end if you don't tell me who did this."

"It was an accident—he was mad that the tips were lower than expected. The night was slow, and I couldn't pull in a lot." I try to look anywhere but at his handsome face. "But you need to let me go."

He scoffs, "An accident? How can someone wrapping their hands around someone's neck be considered an accident?" Wilder's grip tightens, and I can feel the tension radiating off him like heat from a fire. "Arwen, you matter to me, even if I just met you. I can't stand by and let him hurt you."

"I'm not worth saving. You don't even know me," I say, biting back a sob.

He lets me go and runs his hands through his hair, tension practically radiating off his muscular frame. I swallow past the lump in my throat.

"You're mine now."

I look at him like he's crazy and wonder what kind of mind fuck game he's playing with me. *Is it an act to get me to fall into his bed so he can take what he wants? Then what? Dump me at my apartment later tonight and move on to his next piece of ass? What the actual fuck!*

"I'm not yours and I have to get back to work."

"You are, you just haven't realized it yet," he retorts with a clipped tone. "This isn't over, Arwen. He will never lay another finger on you." His threat rings through the air.

Before I can reply the door opens, bringing a blast of warm air as Kit pops her head out and calls, "Break is almost over. I'm sorry. Are you okay?" she asks, looking over my shoulder at the man behind me.

The warmth from Wilder fades as a chill runs through me, reminding me how exposed I am. "Yes. Thank you." I turn to look at Wilder, his stony mask firmly in place, only his golden eyes give him away. I follow Kit inside, leaving this beast of a man behind.

Kit stands behind the bar next to me, passing out drinks as I try to distract myself and pick up more orders.

"Be careful with that one," Kit begins. "I sense a shifter a mile away."

A gasp leaves my throat. *He's a ... shifter?* They aren't necessarily well liked in town. No wonder his eyes were so intense. The color change wasn't an illusion like I'd thought.

"He was ... looking for directions," I lie, my hands trembling with this new knowledge. A glass slips from my fingers, shattering on the floor. A quietness falls over the bar as everyone looks at me.

I rush around the counter and clean the mess, dumping the large pieces into the trash, slicing my hand in the process. Before I realize what's happening, I'm being scooped up by strong muscular arms and carried to the bathroom.

"Hey! What the hell?" I yelp. "Put me down!" He

doesn't answer, just moves swiftly, expertly navigating the cramped corridors of the bar until he pushes open the bathroom door and kicks it shut behind him.

"I said, put me down!"

Wilder finally complies, setting me on the counter next to the tiny sink. "You're bleeding."

He grabs my wrist and examines the small cut.

"It's nothing," I protest, trying to pull away.

"Nothing? You're cut. Besides, you don't get to tell me what to do," he mutters, pulling a first aid kit from beneath the sink. His tone is firm, but there's something tender in the way he handles me.

"Where did you even learn how to patch up a wound? Are you a doctor or something?" I ask, watching him closely. His broad shoulders tense as he focuses on my hand.

"No, just learned a few things along the way."

"And what does that mean?" Wilder glances up at me, his expression softening, the anger from earlier dissipating for a moment.

"I've survived a lot," he says quietly. A thick silence settles in as he cleans my hand, making my heart race for reasons beyond the sting of alcohol.

"Why do you care? I'm just a bartender. There's nothing special about me."

He puts his hand under my chin and tilts my head so that my face meets his gaze. My legs part willingly, a subtle invitation, as he steps closer, wedging me against his solid chest. His eyes linger on my neck, and a shiver works its way down my spine as his hand wraps around my throat—gentle, yet possessive. Nothing like how Jarrod does it. This feels … hot, erotic, forbidden.

Before I fully realize what's happening, his lips are on mine. Electric currents race through my veins, igniting every nerve ending. I feel the desperation of the moment, my heart pounding with adrenaline. This doesn't make any sense and yet I can't make myself pull away. His kisses are firm, and the scruff from his beard creates a delicious friction against my cheeks. He lets out a low groan and bites my lip.

"Fuck, you taste as good as I imagined," he murmurs between kisses.

His lips are raw with passion, but their intensity is underlined by something I can't quite name. Something tempting. It's like the universe planted this man before me purposely, but I stopped believing in fairy tales long ago. No, reality is harsh and deadly.

"S-stop," I whimper. "He'll kill me."

Wilder growls, pulling back just enough to make eye contact. "I told you already. If he hurts you, I will murder him." His voice is low, fierce. He presses his forehead to mine, taking a sharp, labored breath. "I won't let anyone hurt what's mine."

"I'm not yours!" I protest, trying to shove him away, but every fiber of my being resists. The heat between us is intoxicating, and I'm overwhelmed by his advances. Wilder tightens his hold, defiance flickering in his eyes.

"So innocent, so sweet," he murmurs, nuzzling my hair, his hot breath ghosting along the nape of my neck. His teeth graze my skin, sending a thrill coursing through me. He inhales me, like I'm the most precious smelling flower.

"What the hell?" I squirm, flipping around to face him, searching for rationality in his gaze.

"Stop fighting this, Starlight! It's happening. "

"I ... no... We can't—"

"This is not a debate." His voice darkens, filled with a fierce resolve. Wilder's hand is still on my throat, keeping me locked in place as if he's afraid to let me go.

Almost protectively. My heart is brimming with confusion, excitement, and most alarming arousal.

"What do you want from me?" I implore, attempting to decipher the intensity welling in his gaze.

"Everything, Arwen. *Everything.*"

"I have nothing left to give," I whimper. He cups my face, running his thumbs along my cheeks in tantalizing circles. My breath hitches in my chest at the sheer intensity of his gaze. I've never been this close to a shifter before. *Are they all this ... consuming?* I feel like he can see into my soul and it's both terrifying and comforting. Clearly, I'm not in my right frame of mind because nothing about this makes any sense.

"I can't do this!" I slide off the counter and storm out of the bathroom, the sound of my heartbeat echoing desperately in my ears.

"Kit, I need to go," I call out, making her look up with startled eyes.

"Of course, hun. Go, I'll see you next week." She smiles brightly, oblivious to my entire world disintegrating. I don't mention that I probably won't be seeing her again. I've got to get my money and leave tonight.

I grab my purse, almost spilling its contents onto the floor as I rush out the door. Each step feels heavy, and the whole walk home, I feel like I'm being trailed by shadows, an ominous presence lingering behind me. But when I look back, no one's there.

"Just get home," I mutter to myself.

I slip through my front door quietly, praying that Jarrod's asleep on the couch like he normally is at this time. Silence envelops the house.

Maybe he went out? I hope. I rush to the back of my closet and slide the brick aside, revealing my stash—a small fortune I'd been collecting for months, enough to help me vanish. I shove everything else into the duffel bag, fingers trembling as I reach inside, my heart beating frantically.

"Well, well, well. What do we have here?" Jarrod's voice drips with venom, slithering through the stillness like a serpent. I freeze at the sound, recognizing the tone I have learned to dread. I see the crazy look in his eyes that he gets before he attacks.

"What do you want, Jarrod?" I question, trying to keep my voice steady as I slide the bag behind me.

He glances at the wads of cash in the bag and sneers, "You won't be needing that where you're going." He pushes himself off from the wall and stalks toward me, every step a deadly promise. My stomach twists in fear, and I instinctively step back, hitting the wall. I'm trapped.

"You're gonna kill me," I whisper. My breath hitches in my throat as he pulls out a blade, the light glinting off its edge like the fangs of a beast. "Please—"

"You think you can just leave me? After everything I've done for you?" He lunges forward, and I scream, throwing the duffel bag at him in a desperate attempt to buy myself a second.

"Get away from me!" I shout, adrenaline surging as I scramble to grab the heavy lamp off my dresser.

He sidesteps effortlessly. "Pathetic, really." Jarrod laughs, but there's no joy in it, just a predator's glee.

"I will not go back to your hell!" I swing the lamp, catching him off guard, the force knocking him back momentarily. He stumbles, surprise flashing across his face.

"You'll regret that," he growls, bleeding fury as he recovers.

Just as he's about to pounce, there's a loud bang, the sound of the front door splintering open. Large footsteps stomp into the room and I see him, Wilder. His eyes have turned to golden slits as he looks at the scene before him. Everything happens so fast that I stumble onto the ground, curling into myself as I watch the horror play out in front of me.

Chapter Three

Wilder

After the thrilling fight, I didn't want to stay cooped up in my apartment like usual. It has been a while since I'd ventured out of my normal solidarity and to my surprise, I crave it more. I guess the city has been growing on me these past few years. The private elevator doors open to the underground garage, forcing the chill in the air to hit me in the face. I make my way over to my beautiful custom chopper, itching to feel the thrum of the engine beneath me. The adrenaline that courses through me as I ride, rivals the feel of my puma racing through the forest. Being in a large city has its limitations, but at least on the open road I feel free.

I make my way across town, letting the bike lead me. There is no destination in mind but as I pull up to a small dive bar on the outskirts of Manhattan, I decide to park and cut the engine.

The bright pink neon sign, ALLEY KATZ, illuminates the mostly deserted street. I guess I'll take my chances here. I've never heard of it, but if they aren't shifter friendly then I'll see myself out.

As I walk up to the front doors, a large bouncer stands to the side. His scent wafts through the air, and I instantly relax. If they have a shifter as a bouncer then there shouldn't be a problem.

"Evening," I say as I approach. He looks surprised but then relaxes.

"Trying a new spot out tonight?" he asks, looking me over to see if I'm a threat. I don't blame him. My looks scream dangerous, but that's the way I like it. I'd rather people see what I am than hide behind a mask.

"Yeah. Just needed a change of scenery." He nods, holding his clipboard in place.

"Then, welcome to our little slice of hell." He laughs, holding the door open for me.

The moment I walk into the dive bar, I can sense her. My animal beats against my chest, wanting me to unleash him. The air is thick with the scent of sweat, whiskey, and something uniquely hers. I take a seat at the bar, my instincts alive and alert, when I see her—a gorgeous young human and something else I can't place. She stands behind the bar, pouring drinks, and all I can think is, *mine.*

She's mine.

"She's our fated mate," my inner beast growls, his voice a low rumble in my mind. I barely register the words as my gaze falls on her. Everything feels heightened: every movement, every blink of her lashes. It's as if I had been half alive before she entered the frame of my reality. I search her face for any signs of recognition—an eye twitch, a scent shift, anything—but she stays neutral, confusion flickering in her vibrant violet eyes, though it lingers just beneath the surface.

"Whiskey, neat," I finally manage to say. She pours the drink expertly, sliding it toward me with a hint of finesse. The air grows still, everything around us blurring into the background. I stare into her eyes, my heart catching in my chest. Her stunning silver hair cascades over her shoulders in soft waves, and I have to force my hands to remain at my sides, not reaching out to run my fingers through that silky softness.

"What's your name?" I ask, hating the need to know but unable to suppress it. "It's not every day I meet someone as intriguing as you … Starlight." At that, she hesitates, the air shifting between us, electric and charged. My beast paws at my sanity, willing me to make a move.

Finally, she whispers, "My name is Arwen."

The moment the name leaves her lips, shock waves rip through me. I repeat it, "Arwen," committing every syllable to memory. My beast becomes even more agitated now, unwilling to acknowledge the human standing by her side.

"She's too close to that guy," he growls, the sound echoing in my psyche. *"Make her ours."*

Fucking mine.

I glance past Arwen to the man who had been chatting with her. The cocky bastard leans more toward her than necessary, charm oozing from him. I resist the urge to snarl, to mark my territory in the most primal of ways.

"What's he to you?" I ask, my tone sharper than I intended.

Arwen raises her brows in surprise, her lips parting slightly, but I can't read her thoughts. "He's just a regular, harmless guy," she replies, yet the edge in her voice states that there's more beneath the surface.

"Harmless people don't linger, Arwen," I say, my voice low but firm. "He's in your space."

With a deep breath, she takes a step back, her eyes clouded over in thought. "You seem intense," she remarks, a hint of humor gracing her lips, but it's laced with uncertainty. Some other drunk human cozies up beside me, making me want to rip her hands from me. The only person allowed to touch me now is her, Arwen. I see jealousy flash through her eyes briefly before she turns to serve a different customer. For some reason, I love the fact that she didn't like seeing that woman on me. She may not know it, but subconsciously she can feel the same pull as me.

But then my focus shifts and horror grips my

heart as I notice the bruises along her neck, faint but visible under the soft glow of the bar lights. Marks of aggression, remnants of a fool's cowardice. Anger roars to life within me, igniting a fire that demands justice.

I slam my fist down on the bar, earning a few glances from neighboring tables—a rookie mistake. I can see her flinch, tears threatening to spill as she covers her chest with her hand. The sight shatters my resolve.

"I'm sorry. It's time for my break," she murmurs. In a heartbeat, she pulls away, darting outside. Without thinking, my feet move, fueled by the overpowering urge of my beast, demanding possession, a primal instinct that roars louder than any logical thought.

Ours, yes. Arwen is ours to claim.

I follow her into the cold night, the air stirring with tension. I can smell the salt of her tears from a distance, sparking a fury that is as instinctual as it is emotional. She is standing against the brick wall behind the bar, her eyes closed as she sings. As soon as her song fills the air, I feel an immediate change. The melody is hauntingly beautiful, carrying the echoes of the sea and the depth of human emotion. The song is not just beautiful, it is soul-deep, resonating with my very essence. It is as if the universe itself has crafted this song just for me. My heart, which was pounding with the residual adrenaline from her running away from me, begins to slow, each beat synching with the rhythm of her voice.

The turmoil in my heart begins to settle, the grief and anger that have been my constant companions melts away, replaced by a profound sense of peace. My body, still aching from the battle, relaxes as the soothing warmth of her song spreads through me. My puma stirs within, recognizing the connection we share, the bond that goes beyond physical attraction or even emotional connection. This is something deeper, primal, and eternal.

There was something different about her, something I couldn't quite put my finger on, until now. The realization hits me like a bolt of lightning—Arwen isn't just human, she's part siren. She turns her head, hearing me approach, making her song fade away into the night. The loss of the melody brings back the rage I felt when I saw her beautiful, milky flesh marred with another man's brutal attacks.

She's telling me something, but I can barely focus on anything other than the perfection in front of me. Arwen has this natural, flawless beauty that would transcend time. Her silver hair sparkles in the moonlight, that's how Starlight slipped from my lips because she looks like a star on earth. Her beauty is not just in her appearance but in the way she moves, the way she breathes life into every moment.

"Arwen," I breathe, standing before her. My fingers itch to reach out, to pull her close and protect her from the pain that twists her features.

Her gaze meets mine, filled with fear and uncertainty. "It's nothing," she insists, a lie so thin it can shatter with the slightest breath. She bursts into tears and my animal bristles, ready to tear apart the fool who has brought her to this level.

Anger ignites a burning flame within, fueled by her pain. I will do what my beast demands. I will fucking kill the son of a bitch that hurt her, then I'll make her see that I will cherish and keep her safe forever. The thought should fucking terrify me. I swore never again to get involved after Emily, but gods, never in my life would I have ever believed I would find my true mate. If there was any lingering doubt that she was mine, it was crushed the moment I heard her voice.

The vision of her living with another man, laying

down with him every day in bed drives me insane. I won't let that happen. I have to claim her. The beast is thrashing, demanding release.

Fucking hell.

"Don't fucking lie to me," I snap, my voice low and resonant. I step into the encroaching darkness, my shadow swallowing her small frame. Her tears become an electric current surging through me, igniting a burning anger deep within. I feel the primal instinct to protect her surge. The sensation is like a fierce hunger at the bottom of my soul.

"How long?"

"Why do you care?" Her light eyebrows draw together in confusion. The jealousy surges like a dance through my veins. I can feel the beast pushing against my skin, begging to claim her, to mark her, to own her.

"How long, Arwen?" I repeat, the low growl escaping my throat, causing the night to shudder.

"Only a couple of years," she admits, her voice breaking. The surrender in her tone feels like a dagger through my heart. The image of that pathetic bastard, with his filthy hands on her, is like gasoline to a fire. I clench my fists, fighting the urge to unleash the beast within.

I take a step forward, grabbing her by the arms and pulling her to me, the warmth of her body seeping into mine, momentarily calming the raging storm.

"I'll kill him!" I growl, unable to contain the turmoil any longer.

"No, it's my fault," she lies again, her voice a trembling breeze, shoving the guilt back down my throat. My breath catches as she looks up at me, tears pooling in the corners of her eyes. A swell of protectiveness overwhelms my senses.

"You don't understand, do you?" I dare, letting

the anger edge my words. "How dare you lie to me. How dare he lay a finger on you. You don't deserve this!" She shrugs out of my grip, tears streaming down her cheeks, and it feels like every drop is a nail driven through my chest.

"I'm not done, Arwen!" My voice rumbles like thunder and I can hardly recognize the fury in me. It is my puma, it resonates through me, echoing every insecurity, every primal instinct I possess.

"It was just an accident! He was mad that the tips were lower than expected. We were slow that night!" Her voice cracks in distress. I know she is trying to make sense of it, trying to justify the unjustifiable.

Something inside me snaps. I step forward again, my focus narrowing on her. "You know what you need? You need to come with me. You need to let me protect you." Her eyes flare with emotions I can't decipher— fear, uncertainty.

"I have to get back to work," she murmurs, turning away, fighting the thread that connects us. I let her go, but my hands twitch with the need to reclaim her warmth, revisit that solace amid the chaos. I feel this overwhelming need to claim her and take her as far away as I can to a safe place so she can never be hurt again.

****

After our bathroom encounter, I'll do whatever it takes to prove to her that we belong together. The night air is thick with tension as I watch her leave the bar, her figure casting a long shadow in the streetlight. I follow her home, sticking to the edges of the darkness, careful to remain unseen. My instincts tell me she can sense me. She continually turns back, glancing over her shoulder, her senses heightened in my presence.

Arwen.

Her name is like a mantra, and soon she'll

understand why I'm so relentless.

I watch as she ascends the creaking stairs to her almost condemned apartment. Anger billows within me, knowing she's living in such a desperate place, but there's no time to dwell before a piercing scream slices through the air. *Fuck.*

I rush through the entrance. In an instant, I spot him—the man in the bedroom. My heart races as I see Arwen bleeding, and the rage takes over, clouding my mind, taking control. I charge at him.

All I see is red.

Nothing compares to this bloodlust, not a damn thing. A formidable mountain of muscle, I throw my fists into his throat, feeling the satisfying crunch against my knuckles as I begin to press down, intent on ending this. He struggles but it's pathetic, really. I have no doubt he deserves no mercy for the years he's put his hands on her.

"One... Two... Three..." Each press sends shock waves of vengeance through me, his body flailing against my grip, futile against my strength. This motherfucker has no hope.

And then, silence. He's dead in a pool of his own blood.

"*Arwen*!"

Turning ever so slowly, I see her collapsed on the floor behind me. My focus leaves the dead bastard, and it takes a moment to process the look of horror on her beautiful face.

"Oh, God. You ... killed him?"

"Yes."

Her alarm stabs into me, a piercing agony I didn't expect. The fight returns to her as she jumps to her feet to run, panic flooding her face. *No.* I leap forward. *She can't leave.*

"Arwen, he deserved to die for what he did to

you!" My voice is low, shaking with desperation. "For all the years he put his hands on you. He could have fucking killed you in the worst ways!"

She drops back to the floor, trembling, clutching the cash that slipped from her bag. She shakes her head back and forth, denying all reality. Different emotions swirl within me as I stride toward her, pulling her into my arms. She pushes at me at first but eventually gives in.

"Pack a bag. You're coming home with me, Starlight," I whisper into the shell of her ear.

Her face contorts in disbelief at my words. Her tears stop as if the world has flipped on its axis, and her eyes turn blank, empty.

"I-I don't even know you! And you're a-a…"

"Shifter," I finish for her, the truth crashing between us. She nods, her treasury of emotions spilling into a flash of fear.

She flinches from me, her eyes wide with shock. *Fuck. How could I be so stupid? I'm not just a stranger, I'm a beast, a monster.* At least that's what she thinks. She doesn't know I'd rather die than hurt any part of her.

"I would never hurt you, Arwen." I clutch her tight to my chest, willing her to understand, but instead she tenses against me. When I loosen my grip, she drops to her knees, breaking out in sobs as the realization sinks in.

"He's dead. He's dead. Oh, God, Jarrod's dead." Her disjointed words struggle against the weight of her grief.

"Come on. There's nothing here for you. I'm taking care of you now." Her sobbing ceases. She narrows her eyes, the steel coming back into her gaze.

"And if I want to stay?"

Anger floods my being, my fingers clamping around her arms, eliciting a pained gasp. "That is not happening."

Tension fills the air. I'm too intense, and I know it. The moment changes, and dominating the next breath, I loosen my grip, rubbing the red marks along her arms.

"Shit, Arwen, I'm sorry." I bring her face closer, capturing her trembling lips with my own. Locking onto her, I murmur, "Baby, please come home with me." In that moment, our fear and pain intermingle as she responds, and she kisses me back. I nip at her plump bottom lip, and she groans in submission.

"There's something I need to tell you," I begin as I pull back from her, needing to see into her eyes.

"What is it?" she asks hesitantly, as if I'm about to drop another emotional bomb on her and maybe I am. Who knows how she will react to this news.

I reach out and take her hands in mine, the warmth of her skin igniting something deep within me.

"From the moment we met, I felt an inexplicable connection to you. It was more than just attraction or friendship. It's a bond that runs deeper, something primal and undeniable."

Her eyes are wide, confusion and intrigue swirling in those pools of violet. "What do you mean?"

I take a deep breath, feeling the gravity of my words. "I mean that we're fated mates," I explain slowly. "In our world, fated mates are destined for one another, bound by a bond that transcends time and space. It's why I feel such a strong pull toward you, why I can't imagine my life without you." Arwen's eyes widen and she opens her mouth to speak but then closes it again. I can see the questions swirling through her mind.

"Fated mates?" she repeats, disbelief tinged with curiosity. "What do you mean 'our world'? I'm not a shifter."

A pang of guilt washes over me. *How the hell*

does this beautiful soul not know what she is? And why of all people do I have to be the one to tell her? On top of everything else, she's likely to either not believe me or go into shock. Neither are viable options.

"I understand how shocking this must be. You've always felt different, right? Like there's something more beneath the surface?" I pause, watching her closely. "Our world isn't just about shifters. It's a world of hidden magic and extraordinary beings. Being a shifter is just one part of it."

Arwen blinks, her expression a mix of disbelief and curiosity. "But … I've never shifted. I don't feel like a shifter."

I nod. "You're right. You're not a shifter, but you're part of this world in your own unique way. Your song, your ability to soothe and heal—it's your siren heritage. Part siren, part human. It's a rare and powerful combination." I let my words sink in before continuing. "Has anyone ever told you they didn't like your singing? Or has it ever made you feel differently?"

"I guess I've had moments where I felt like I could calm someone just by … you know, singing to them." She pauses, expression shifting. I can see the memories flashing in her mind like a film reel, piecing together a puzzle she never knew existed. "Jarrod hated it."

"Your voice carries magic, a gift from your siren lineage. And it's also why we're fated mates. Our bond goes beyond being shifters, it's about our souls finding each other." Her gasp echoes against the wooden walls, an audible acknowledgment of realization as she inches closer to me.

"So, you're saying I'm part of this hidden world too?"

"Yes, and it means you have a strength and power

you've only begun to discover." Arwen shakes her head slowly.

Her brow furrows. "I don't have power. If I did, then…" she trails off, clutching her throat, the air almost thick with disbelief. "This can't be real. I've lived my whole life thinking I was ordinary. How could I possibly be part of this world without knowing it? What makes you think I can and will trust you? Do you see what I've been through?" She points to the lifeless body on the floor behind us. "And you want me to just automatically trust you?"

"Sometimes, our true nature takes time to reveal itself," I say gently. "It could be your connection to me has triggered the awakening of your powers. Our bond is strong, and it's bringing out the best in both of us."

Her anger flashes, clenched fists shaking. "Why now? Why am I finding out about this only now?"

"Because sometimes the universe works its own timing. Sometimes, even when we don't believe we're special, we are meant for greatness. Your affinity for singing, the way your voice soothes the troubled souls around you, it all connects back to your lineage. Your mother must've been a siren."

Tears pool in her eyes, and I rush to comfort her. She shakes her head vehemently. "I wouldn't know. I never knew my parents!"

My gaze softens as I look at Arwen, understanding her confusion and disbelief. I take a deep breath, searching for the right words to convey the depth of what I feel.

"I know it's painful, and I know this is a lot to process. But it's true. The signs were there, waiting for you to uncover them. Think—your voice, the way it carries emotion. It's a gift!"

As we stand there, the hazy remnants of the past

cling to the air like smoke. Arwen takes a deep breath, searching my eyes for anything that will hint at deception. "So, you mean to say that my silence over these past years was just waiting on the other side of this revelation?"

I nod, feeling the bond between us grow, a dance of energies intertwining. "It is entirely possible. Your powers might amplify with time, as our heartbeats draw closer together. When I first saw you, it wasn't just a passing glance. I felt an inexplicable power. Something inside me recognized something deep within you—a connection that has always existed, even if hidden from your sight." I brush a strand of her silvery hair behind her ear, feeling a magnetic pull between us.

"Your presence soothes me, your voice heals me, and it's as if you've awakened a part of me I didn't know was asleep."

Arwen's eyes are wide, her breaths shallow as she tries to process my words. "But how can you be so sure?" Her eyebrows draw up in confusion.

"It's hard to explain, but it's not just about feelings. There are signs, a sense of completeness when we're together. My puma reacts to you in ways it never has with anyone else. And your song resonates with my very being. This is more than mere attraction or affection—it's destiny."

"So, you're a puma?" she asks quietly. I nod, a hint of a smile playing on my lips.

"I know it's a lot to take in, and I understand if you're scared or uncertain. But I promise, this bond is real, and it's something we'll explore and understand together. I'll be here every step of the way, Arwen. We're meant to be, and I'll do everything to prove it to you." I hold her gaze, never wavering.

"I did feel something when I first met you. It was

strange. I can't explain it," she admits, an ember of resolve starting to glow within her.

"You're mine, Starlight." My voice is filled with unwavering certainty. "If you try to run, I will chase your ass down and drag you to my penthouse." I growl low, every word a promise, raw and unyielding. A shiver runs through her, though not from fear. I catch the scent of arousal blooming like a flower in the night as she looks up at me, her feet dancing back and forth like she is primed for flight or fight. Her violet eyes glimmer with something new, something hopeful.

She glances around the shabby apartment, eyes flitting to the body lying on the ruined floor, and then finally back to me. She takes a deep breath, and when she speaks, it's barely above a whisper.

"Okay."

Chapter Four

Arwen

I begin throwing things into a bag, wondering what I even want to bring. I don't want any reminders of this shattered life. I want what Wilder is promising—a new start. He saved me tonight in more ways than one. I've always been different, and he's given me the gift of knowledge, of what I am and what I can become.

Wilder walks back into my room as I'm stuffing things into my bag. He slips his phone in his pocket then leans against the door, watching me. Chills run through me at his hard gaze. I can't describe it. He's so intoxicating, like a new drug I never knew I needed but I can never live without.

"Someone will be here soon to clean up this mess," he says coolly, like this is a normal occurrence for him and maybe it is.

"Will you get in trouble?" I ask, suddenly worried.

"No. There's an agency called Shifter Relations that specializes in crime scene cleanups. Once they sweep through here, it will be like it never happened. And I'm sure no one will miss the bastard," he growls the last part as if he's still angry with him even though he's dead.

I can't believe there is this whole world I didn't know about. I mean, I knew about shifters but that's the extent of my knowledge and I definitely didn't know there were so many. My mind is reeling from all the information that's been thrown at me tonight.

He pulls the bag from my hands, throwing it over his shoulder as he takes my hand to pull me along with him.

"Time to go home, baby," he murmurs in my ear.

Home. I've never felt like I knew what that word meant until Wilder. This man …well, shifter, stormed into my life, turning everything upside down. I still feel like I'll wake up tomorrow and everything will have been a fever dream.

As we walk, the neon lights of the bar dim in the distance, replaced by the comforting glow of street lamps illuminating the sidewalk. The air has a chill to it, a stark contrast to the heat of the moment we just shared back inside. My heart still races, filled with confusion and exhilaration, as I steal glances at him. His jaw is clenched, a brow arched with concern.

"What are you thinking about, Starlight?" he asks, softer than I expect. His brow is furrowed, concern etched into the lines of his ruggedly gorgeous face.

"I don't know, it's just … tonight, everything has changed. I can't go back to the way things were. I don't want to."

He stops suddenly, pulling me closer with both hands on my shoulders. "You won't have to. You're with me now."

"Yeah, but you're a shifter, Wilder. What if I don't fit into your world?" I ask, still grappling with the idea.

He cracks a smile, though his eyes remain serious. "You're all wrong, Arwen. You fit perfectly, like the moon does with the tide. We'll find our rhythm."

"Why would you even want me?" The question spills out before I can stop it, my voice trembling as tears threaten to spill. The insecurities Jarrod drilled into me are ever present and I don't feel like I'm good enough for anyone.

"Because you're extraordinary," he replies without hesitating, his gaze unwavering. "I lost my way for far too long, and then you crashed into my life, and I realize it's you I need. I never knew fated mates were real, but I've never been more certain of anything in my life."

I nestle against him, closing my eyes and allowing myself to believe. The shadows in my past fade as a spark ignites my soul. Maybe Wilder was right. Home wasn't a place, it was never meant to be. It was a feeling, and I had finally found it in his embrace.

He leads me to a huge black motorcycle with "WB" inscribed on the side. My eyes widen with awe at the vehicle gleaming under the moonlight.

"Is this yours?" I ask incredulously, my voice barely a whisper.

"Yeah. Like it?" he replies, a grin forming on his lips.

"It's nicer than anything I've ever seen." I can't help but feel inferior in my corset and jeans, standing beside this machine of power and elegance. "Are you wealthy or something?"

Wilder chuckles, the sound deep and rich, like velvet wrapping around a wooden chair. "It's just a motorcycle. Don't let it scare you. I am definitely not your average rich guy."

I raise an eyebrow at his contradiction. "Is there such a thing as an average rich guy?"

He smirks, leaning against the motorcycle with a casual grace. "I guess it's all about how you define 'average.' But genuinely, wealth isn't what matters."

I smirk back, letting a playful tone surface, "Then what does?"

Wilder steps closer, worlds between us melting as he bridges that gap. His breath is warm against my face, sending shivers down my spine. "Connection. Trust. That spark."

My breath catches in my throat as the moment lingers, almost reverent. "And what if it fades?" I don't know why the thought terrifies me. Perhaps it's the sudden pull I feel toward him.

"Can fated mates tire of one another?" He raises an eyebrow, a teasing glint dancing in his mesmerizing yellow eyes.

"I don't know, can they?" I bite my lip, torn between jest and seriousness, the weight of his words pressing against the rib cage of my hope.

"Not if it's genuine." His tone is steady, almost commanding, and a warmth radiates within my chest. "Arwen, you're my other half. I promise I'll always fight for us."

I visibly relax, letting his words wash over me like morning sunlight after a cool night. There's determination in his gaze, a promise so powerful it nearly glows. "Okay," I finally manage, though doubt still lingers.

"Okay?" he echoes, a grin spreading across his face.

"Yeah, just…" I look down at my chubby body then look at his perfect chiseled physique. My heart races in my throat. He could have anyone he wants.

Wilder doesn't flinch. Instead, he reaches out and gently tucks a strand of hair behind my ear, the tenderness of his touch shooting warmth through my body. "Arwen, you're the most gorgeous creature I've ever seen. Inside and out. Trust me."

I feel myself blush, the night's atmosphere shifting from uncertain tension to something warm and inviting. "I guess we'll see how far that trust goes, won't we?"

"Are you ready to ride?" His expression turns serious, eyes locking onto mine, expectations brewing in the air like a thunderstorm brewing behind a window.

"Ready? I've never ridden a motorcycle before. What if I fall?"

He leans closer, his voice lowering to a conspiratorial whisper. "Then I'll catch you, I promise."

I hesitate only for a moment before climbing onto the seat, a tingle of exhilaration replacing my fear. He gently places a helmet over my head, pulling the chin strap tight as if to ensure my safety. I can smell his leather jacket—an intoxicating mix of musky scent and adventure—as he shrugs out of it and drapes it over my shoulders.

"Here, put this on. I don't want you to get a chill," he says, his voice low and smooth, wrapping around me like a spell.

I chuckle nervously, trying to hide the way my heart flips as Wilder's fingers brush against my arms. "If I freeze, it'll be from fear, not cold!"

He grins, a cocky glint in his eyes. "Then hold on tight."

With a roaring engine, Wilder brings the bike to life, the vibrations transmitting through my body. As we surge forward, the world blurs—a kaleidoscope of city lights and swirling shadows.

"What do you think?" Wilder shouts over the wind, the exhilaration in his voice cutting through my initial apprehension.

"I think it's amazing!" I shout back, laughter bubbling up as the wind rushes past us. The streets open like a pathway through the dark, leading to places I have never imagined going. My heart thunders in my chest, a rhythm that matches the purr of the bike racing through my veins.

But buried beneath the thrill is a deeper, more primal need. Suddenly, I am achy and yearning for

Wilder in a way I never thought I would want a man again. A longing as potent as the magic I feel buzzing in the air. I clench my thighs against his sides, hoping the friction will douse the insatiable fire building within me. But instead, it only intensifies the energy between us.

"Keep doing that, Starlight," he growls, molten desire lacing his tone, wrapping around me like an embrace, "and we won't make it back to my penthouse before I have to stop and bend you over this bike to pound into that pussy."

His words stoke the flames of my desire, igniting my senses in a way I had long since forgotten.

Every thrust of the bike's engine synchronizes with the pounding in my chest, each twist in the road mirroring the spirals of my yearning. The night teems with possibilities, and with Wilder's warm laughter and whispered promises chasing the wind, I feel like I am unearthing a part of myself I thought was lost.

Taking in a sharp breath of exhilarating freedom, I turn and wrap my arms tighter around his torso, surrendering myself completely to this wild ride and to him. The city lights dance around us like ethereal spirits, urging us toward an adventure that feels both dangerous and deliciously inevitable.

Chapter Five

Wilder

By the time we pull into my private parking garage, I'm feral with need. Arwen's thighs rubbing against me and the delicious smell of her pussy has been the ultimate torture. The soft hum of the engine fades as I cut the ignition, but the heat between us ignites, palpable and raw, buzzing like electric energy.

She's a fantasy, an exquisite beauty with hair like molten silver. Even in the dim light, her violet eyes glint with a mischievous spark that promises secrets, adventure, and desire.

I swing off the bike and pull her from the seat, feeling that delightful warmth radiating from her body as I back her against the sleek metal wall of the garage. Arwen gasps, a sound so sweet it only fuels my need further. Every curve of her body feels electric against mine, and I drink in her soft moans, devouring the way she trembles under my hands.

"You make me lose my mind, you know that?" I whisper, intoxicated by her presence.

Her breath quickens as I draw closer, my lips hovering inches from her own. Arwen's lips part ever so slightly, an invitation that pulls me in like a moth to a flame. There's a wildness in her that matches my own, an ancient spirit that seems to pulse just beneath the surface. I can feel it in my bones, a vibrant dance of primal energy that thrums in our air.

"Then take me," she purrs, her voice low and sultry, as intoxicating as wine.

"More," I growl, my lips trailing down the exquisite line of her throat, tasting the sweet pulse beneath the soft skin, my hunger pressing harder. Arwen's fingers weave through my hair, tugging me closer, urging me on. She wants this just as badly as I do, her need matching mine, creating a symphony of lust that resonates with our very souls.

With one swift move, I pick her up, her legs wrapping around my waist, as if she was made to fit me. I stride toward the elevator, her body fitting to mine like a second skin, the sound of her laughter ringing in my ears like music.

After pressing the button, the doors slide open and I slam her against the wall, the cool metal contrasting with the heat of our bodies. I can't contain myself any longer, and I crash my lips down on hers, the kiss igniting with urgency as I explore her mouth, tasting the sweet nectar of her need.

The elevator climbs, the numbers flickering on the panel as we lose ourselves in each other's embrace.

"You're so much, Arwen," I breathe against her lips, the air thick with what we both crave.

"Then let's make this worth it," she breathes back, her voice a siren song that pulls me deeper into the abyss of our mutual desire. Her arms tighten around my neck, pulling me closer as if she can sense the fraying edges of my control.

With another surge of passion, I pull back slightly to look into her enchanting eyes. The dim light of the elevator casts a soft glow around her, highlighting the delicate points of her cheekbones, the way her lips are slightly swollen from our fervent kiss. My heart races, not just from the heat between us but from the wild wonder of having her here, now.

"Do you want me to stop?" I manage to ask, a playful challenge in my tone, knowing full well my body screams otherwise, my heart alive with the rhythm of our shared desires.

"Never. Just more of this … more of us." She exhales, and I see the fire in her gaze, sensing that she's ready to leap into this dangerous dance.

Our connection surges like a wild storm as I stumble out of the elevator, the world outside fading away. I lead her toward the expansive living room, the luxurious furnishings momentarily forgotten as I become entranced by the woman in my arms. Every curve, every shiver of her body against mine promises uncharted territory, and I yearn to explore it all.

I carry her to *our* bedroom. The plush king-sized bed awaits us, cloaked in the scent of soft linen and desire. She lays on the bed, sparkling beneath the muted light, her eyes like glowing embers, a predator anticipating the thrill of the chase.

I hover over her, an unquenchable thirst surging through me—a need that seems to pulse in tandem with the rapid beat of my heart. As I lean in, brushing my lips against her collarbone, the taste of her sweet skin stirs something primal within. My fingers caress the curve of her hip, eliciting a soft gasp that reverberates in my ears.

"Tell me what you want," I rasp, my voice saturated with longing.

"I want to feel every part of you," she replies, her gaze fierce and heavy with expectation.

With an exhilarated growl, I draw back momentarily, capturing her mouth in a fierce kiss, pouring everything into that moment. Our bodies tangle together, each kiss and caress weaving us into an inseparable union—a tapestry of raw emotion and desire.

Arousal simmers dangerously beneath the surface, a boiling tempest threatening to explode. I can feel her innocence fading, replaced by the challenge that radiates from the depths of her being.

In a spontaneous burst of energy, I rip my shirt from my body, not caring as the fabric tears and falls to the floor. My hands fall to her clothes, not taking gentle care in their removal as I tear away the barriers that separate us. Each shred becomes a reminder of the world we were shedding, leaving only urgency and anticipation in their wake.

Her shocked gasps ignite a deeper hunger within me. The thrill of taking what is rightfully mine fuels my desires, raw and unabashed.

"Then say it. Say you're fucking mine, and when we're alone that body is for me!" I demand, the words spilling from my lips like a guttural promise.

The air grows thick, electricity crackling between us as I restrain myself, my body aching to thrust into her, to claim her completely. I restrain my desire, reveling in the way her body responds to me, her sweet pussy already glistening, leaving evidence of our heated connection.

"Are you afraid of the challenge my cock poses, the claim it needs to make to your hot, tight pussy?" I taunt, my fingers dancing across her swollen lips, teasingly dipping between them. "Ah. I knew this pussy would look beautiful. Tight and swollen, pink and juicy."

Arwen's breath hitches, a wild spark ignites in her gaze. She writhes beneath me, the anticipation mirrored in the way her body opens up, yearning for exploration and binding. I am as consumed as she is, lost to an intoxicating mix of passion and hunger.

"Say it, Starlight," I growl, the words pouring from my lips in a low, possessive whisper. My inner puma, ever protective, needs to hear it as much as it needs to breathe.

"Yes," she whimpers, her voice soft yet firm, a beautiful melody in the cacophony of our desires. "I'm yours, Wilder."

The confirmation sends shivers down my spine. In that moment, we transcend into something more—two celestial bodies colliding in a blaze of passion that threatens to swallow us whole. A primal sound erupts from within me, echoing in the still night, as I finally surrender to the tempest—a storm of flesh and fire, exploration and abandonment.

I crawl down her body, my lips nipping and licking every luscious curve, my hunger growing more insatiable with each taste of her silky skin. She is pure perfection. She pulls me closer even as she lays beneath me, her sweet gasps fueling my fervor.

I want to worship her until she realizes she's the only thing I desire. Now. Forever. She's mine—to cherish and to own.

I flatten myself against the bed, my face level with her dripping cunt, inhaling the most exquisite scent. She is like the rarest fruit in the world. My tongue darts out, hunger consuming me as I finally taste her essence. The sweetness washes over my senses, sending shock waves through my body as I hear her moan in pleasure.

"Wilder..." she breathes, her voice thick with yearning, the syllables vibrating like a spell upon her lips. The way she calls my name, a whisper laced with submission, fuels the deep-seated primal urge within me.

"Say my name again," I demand, my voice a rough whisper, the urgency curling through me as I feast upon her soft folds. I can feel her body arching, her thighs urging me deeper, begging for more of my touch, spurring me on. *How could I deny her?*

Her fingers tangle in my hair, guiding my mouth, urging me closer and closer to fervent release. I savor every quiver and sigh from her, losing myself in the taste of her as I plunge into an exquisite rhythm. I want her mind as much as I want her body, to imprint myself on her very soul.

"Wilder," she gasps again, more desperate now, and that sound compels me. I push my tongue deeper, feeling her muscles tighten around my every move. That sweet tension builds, a beautiful tension—a tight pressure reminiscent of the world we are leaving behind.

I can see us there—two celestial bodies, entwined and igniting in flames, spinning in a dizzying dance, lost in dark matter. She tugs me closer at each crest of pleasure the universe has conspired to bring us to this moment.

I can't hold on any longer. I crave connection, I relish in the fire we create. The moment is upon us, and I will take everything, every rich flavor of Arwen, that delicate essence that is now intricately woven with my very being.

One of my fingers slips inside her, stretching, filling her perfectly, heavenly warmth enveloping me. I work the rhythm, torn between the desire to take all of her and show her how tenderness serves our passion as much as lust does.

"Tell me, tell me what you want, Arwen," I murmur against her slick skin, a demand and an offer, colliding with the intensity of our stars in this dark expanse. My fingertips dance still, teasing, evoking gasps that linger in the space between need and want. I crave her voice—a direction to guide me deeper into her universe.

"I want..." she breathes, her eyes reflecting the firelight, the embodiment of every desire woven into her whispered confession, a starburst of vulnerability and raw need. "I want you to claim me, Wilder. Completely. Give me all of you."

The air pulses, thickening with a new heat as I

submit to her wishes. In that moment, I know I will hold nothing back. She is not just my obsession, she is the very core of my existence, and as I rise to meet her fiery gaze, I promise her everything.

I lean up, gathering her juices in my hand, the enticing scent of her arousal filling my senses. I stroke my cock, relishing the friction as her eyes widen in surprise. For a fleeting moment, panic flickers across her beautiful features.

"Wilder, that won't—"

"It will," I interject, tone low and commanding. "You will take everything I give you. I'm going to breed this tight cunt, claim it now and forever. You are bound to me forever, my little Starlight." I groan, pressing the tip against her tight entrance, sensing her heart race beneath my palm. "Fuck, baby. I'm not going to be able to go slow. I need you desperately."

A shiver courses through Arwen's body as she looks deep into my eyes, every worry melting away in the heat of our desires.

"Then take me, Wilder!" she urges, a plea laced with lust and bravery.

With a growl, I press forward, feeling her body yield to me, warm and welcoming, as I sink deeper. Each inch is a revelation, a new frontier of pleasure and connection, until we are finally united, bodies entwined, souls fused.

I lose myself in her heat, in the exquisite sensation of claiming her as mine. I thrust forward, a powerful rhythm intensifying with each movement, hearts pulsing in sync with the ancient magic around us. Arwen cries out, her voice like music in the night air, urging me onward, deeper, faster.

"More, Wilder! I need more!" She writhes beneath me, her body igniting every dormant ember inside me, fueling my urgency.

"You'll have more, baby. I swear it!" I trace my fingers down her supple flesh, marveling at how each touch brings forth a soft gasp or a beautiful whimper.

Without missing a beat, I throw her leg over my shoulder, adjusting our angle to hit deeper, eliciting a scream of pleasure that reverberates in the air—a melody of our wild connection. My thumb circles her clit, a frantic rhythm that matches the powerful thrusts surging from my hips. I want her to come with me, to feel the electric pull of our shared climax. The thought of seeing her swollen with my child sends me spiraling toward new heights of bliss.

"Gods, Arwen! You feel so good!" I grit out, lost in the sensations of her body enveloping mine, the kiss of old magic twirling around in our depths, urging us on, closer to the precipice.

"Yes! Yes! More!" she cries again, and I obey, drowning in the heady mix of lust and longing that binds us together.

I thrust harder, faster, each movement becoming an act of devotion, a prayer to the ancient powers that connect us. Our bodies become a blur, a fusion of rhythm and sighs, the tender space between us collapsing until there's nothing left but raw, unspeakable need.

My puma surges within me, raw instinct igniting a spark in my soul. *Bite her, now. Make the bond permanent.* The call of my primal nature blends seamlessly with my human desires, and I growl, feeling the urge surge through my veins. Arwen's leg slips effortlessly from my shoulder onto the bed, and with a hankering appetite, I crash my lips down on hers.

There is magic in that kiss—a heady concoction of lust and love that threatens to eclipse everything else. I thrust my tongue deep, forcing our flavors together, and she whimpers in delight, clawing at my shoulders, pulling me closer as if she is casting a spell of her own. I welcome the pain. It is a reminder that this was real, that *we* are real.

"Come for me, Arwen," I growl, my fingers digging into her hips as I pull her down onto my cock. "Come with me." Her cries soar to new heights as my teeth sink into the tender flesh of her neck, feeling her pulse quicken beneath my mouth, marking her as mine in every way possible.

As the wave of bliss crashes down upon us, I feel her body tighten around me, pulling me deeper into her warmth. My vision blurs with pleasure, and as I succumb to that euphoric release, I can only think of how she has imprinted herself on my soul.

"I want you carrying my child," I groan. The words tear from my lips in a strangled whisper, sending a thrilling jolt of excitement coursing through me. The primal satisfaction is overwhelming, a truth that can't be denied.

"Yes," she breathes, her body trembling beneath mine, echoing my desires and amplifying the bond that has formed between us.

I surrender fully to the euphoria of our shared existence. I am lost in the bliss of our connection, the overpowering need to fuse our destinies forever. With every thrust, I pour my very essence into her, a promise that transcends the mere act of physical union.

In the crescendo of our passion, I feel the universe shift, the world around us dissolving into nothingness, leaving only the mesmerizing dance of our entwined souls. We are bound for an eternity, intertwined like the vines of the enchanted forest, growing together through seasons of love and desire. I claimed my Starlight completely. *Mine.*

VOLUME THREE

Chapter Six

Arwen

I wake to the sounds of soft snores in my ear. For a moment I freeze, believing Jarrod climbed in bed with me at some point during the night, but then I feel Wilder's large calloused hand run along my belly and over my breasts. A small moan slips from my lips, prompting him to pull me flush against his heated flesh. His hard cock is snuggled into my ass and all the memories from last night come flooding back into my mind. The way his golden eyes darkened when he came inside me, whispering dirty things, like wanting to breed me. My skin flushes and my heart beats erratically in my chest.

"Good morning, Starlight," he murmurs into the shell of my ear before he nibbles his way down my neck and over my shoulder.

"Morning," I breathe as my nipples pebble from his touch.

"Mmm, someone woke up thinking naughty things," he muses as he flips me onto my back and leans over me. His beautiful, messy black hair falls into his face, begging me to run my hands through it. The sun filters through the windows, illuminating the majestic ink covering Wilder's body. My eyes drift over each piece, trying to get a better sense of the man above me.

"Your tattoos," I say softly, running my fingers along the black lines. "What do they mean?"

Wilder follows my gaze, a small, almost imperceptible smile forming on his lips. "Each one tells a part of my story," he begins, "they remind me of who I am and where I've been."

He raises his arm, showing me the detailed portrait of a puma on his upper arm. "This one represents my shifter nature. The puma is my other half, my strength, my protector. It's a part of me that I carry with pride." The animal's sleek, powerful form is captured so vividly it almost feels alive. The puma's eyes are intense, almost as if they're looking straight into my soul.

My eyes then travel to the intricate geometric patterns that wrap around his forearm. "These patterns mimic the fluidity and grace of a puma in motion," he explains. "They're intertwined with elements of nature—leaves, waves—to symbolize my connection to the wild and the natural world. It's a reminder of the balance I strive to maintain between my human and animal sides."

He turns slightly, showing me the trail of paw prints across his shoulder blade. "These paw prints," he says, his voice taking on a darker, more somber tone, "represent my journey. But it's not just any journey. Each step marks a significant moment in my life, a path filled with loss and struggle." I nod, understanding all too well the path of darkness. Something in his pained expression gives me the eerie feeling that he's not telling me about a very important part of his life.

"What happened?" I whisper, needing to know but scared all the same.

Wilder's eyes darken, and for a moment, he seems lost in the memory. He takes a deep breath, his expression wounded but resolute. "I lost someone very close to me," he says quietly, his voice barely above a whisper. "My wife. She was everything to me, and when she died it broke something inside of me."

A heavy silence hangs between us as his words sink in. *A wife? He was married? How old is Wilder?*

"W-was she your mate, too?" I ask as tears pool in the corners of my eyes. *Am I just a replacement? Was she who he was meant to be with?*

Wilder's eyes widen slightly at my question, and I can see the storm of emotions raging within him.

"No, she wasn't my fated mate," he answers softly, his voice filled with a mixture of sorrow and conviction. "We had an arranged marriage. It was something our families decided for us. At first, it was out of duty and respect for our families' wishes. But over time, I did grow to love her deeply. Our bond was built on shared experiences and mutual care, but it wasn't the same as a fated mate bond."

He gently wipes away a tear that escapes down my cheek, his touch warm and reassuring. "You are not a substitute, Arwen. What we have, what I feel for you, is unlike anything I've ever known. It's something deeper, more profound. I know it's hard to believe, especially with everything I've told you, but you are the one I'm meant to be with." Confusion swirls in my mind. *How did he…?* As if sensing my bewilderment, Wilder leans down and presses a kiss to my forehead. It's sweet and tender, a foreign feeling for me.

"You knew what I was thinking," I murmur, the statement half-question, half-wonder.

Wilder's gaze softens as he pulls back slightly, his eyes locking onto mine with an intensity that takes my breath away. "It's part of being fated mates," he says softly. "We have a connection that goes beyond words. It's like our souls are intertwined, allowing us to sense each other's emotions, thoughts, and even fears."

I blink, trying to comprehend the depth of what he's saying. "So, you can read my mind?" I ask, my voice trembling with a mix of awe and trepidation.

"Not exactly," Wilder replies, shaking his head slightly. "It's more like a heightened sense of awareness. I can feel your emotions, sense your hesitations, understand your unspoken thoughts. It's as if there's an invisible thread that connects us, guiding us toward each other."

"Why can't I do that with you?" Fear grips at my chest. Maybe he was wrong about us. All the beautiful promises he's made seem like they may be out of my reach.

"Arwen, it's okay," he soothes. "Our bond is still new, and it takes time for both of us to fully connect on that level. It doesn't mean the connection isn't there or that I'm wrong about us. It's a journey, one we're just beginning."

He cups my chin, his thumb stroking my cheek. "You'll start to sense my thoughts and emotions more clearly as our bond strengthens. It's not something that happens overnight. It's like learning to walk together in perfect sync. It takes patience and trust."

His words hang in the air, a fragile promise I desperately want to believe. The pain and fear in my heart begin to ease just a little, replaced by a glimmer of hope. "I just … I don't want to be second best," I whisper, my voice trembling. "I've never felt like this and I'm scared it's going to end in disaster just like the rest of my life has. It's been a dumpster fire since I was born." I try to look away from his handsome face, the pain in my chest is overwhelming.

Wilder's grip on me tightens, grounding me and forcing my eyes to meet his. "Starlight," he begins. "You are not second best. You are my fated mate, and that makes you my first, my one, my only." He presses his lips to mine in a searing kiss then pulls away. "And I will remind you every fucking day until you finally believe it."

He lifts my chin again, the intensity in his gaze is almost too much to bear, but I'm transfixed by him and I can't look away. "Your past doesn't define you," he continues, his words like a balm to my wounded heart. "I know you've been through hell, but that doesn't mean your future has to be the same. We are stronger together, and I will do everything in my power to ensure that our future is filled with love and happiness."

Tears blur my vision, but I can see the sincerity in his eyes. "I've seen the dumpster fire that life can be," he admits, his own pain flickering in his gaze. "But I've also seen the beauty that can rise from the ashes. You are that beauty, Arwen. You are the light that I never knew I needed."

"Thank you," I whisper.

"You don't ever have to thank me, Starlight." He lays down pulling me with him. As my head rests on his chest, I trace the outlines of his tattoos once more.

"You're very wise," I whisper, wishing I didn't sound like an insecure child.

He chuckles, the sound a low rumble that vibrates beneath my cheek. "Well, I've been around the sun a few times. Seen a thing or two."

"How many times have you been around the sun?" My words come out almost too fast, desperation clawing at me to understand him better. *Will he think I am too young? Too innocent?* At twenty-two, I feel like a fledgling in a world where he has soared for what feels like centuries.

He pauses, his breath steady and thoughtful. "Let's just say... I've counted enough moons to know that age is just a number," he replies, a smile illuminating his face. My chest swells with something that feels a lot like hope.

"But—" I hesitate, feeling the weight of our differences. "I mean ... you're older than me. I don't want you to think..."

His finger lifts, gently resting against my lips to hush my worries. "Arwen, I'm only thirty-nine, not a hundred," he laughs, the sound so contagious it makes my worries melt away.

"Oh." I sigh, relief washing over me like a gentle tide.

"I want one," I murmur. "I always have," I confess as I resume tracking his tattoos under my fingers.

Wilder's arms tighten around me protectively as we lay there. His steady heartbeat is a soothing rhythm beneath my ear, grounding me in this moment.

"Really?" he asks softly, his voice vibrating through his chest.

I nod, tracing the intricate designs on his forearm with my fingertips. "Yes. I've always wanted a tattoo," I murmur. "Something meaningful, something that tells a part of my story, like yours do."

He tilts his head slightly to look down at me, a thoughtful expression on his face. "What kind of tattoo would you get?"

I ponder the question for a moment, my fingers still absently following the lines of his tattoos. "Maybe something that symbolizes strength and resilience," I say finally. "Something that reminds me of where I've been, but also where I'm going. Like a phoenix rising from the sea, since that's where I began."

Wilder's eyes light up with a mixture of admiration and curiosity. "A phoenix rising from the sea," he repeats thoughtfully. "That sounds perfect. You need to embrace your siren origins."

He gently caresses my cheek, his touch soothing and reassuring. "Your siren heritage is a part of you, Arwen. It's not just about where you came from, but also the strength and resilience you've shown despite everything. Embracing it means honoring your past and allowing it to shape the strong, amazing person you've become." I snuggle into him further, allowing his warmth to caress my battered soul. I can already feel the cracks healing with him near, like he's been the glue I needed all along to piece myself together.

A loud ringing blares through the room, making me jolt up from the bed. "Calm down, baby. It's just my phone," he chuckles, as he reaches over to the nightstand to retrieve the device. My heartbeat begins to slow, but I take the opportunity to duck into his adjoining bathroom while he talks.

The bathroom is just as luxurious as his bedroom. I've never seen anything like it. The white and black marble countertop has speckles of gold mixed in making the whole place look so opulent. *What the hell does Wilder do for a living?* A sinking feeling of dread snakes around my throat until I feel like I'm suffocating.

I lean against the cool counter, trying to regain my composure. Taking a deep breath, I look into the mirror. My reflection surprises me—my eyes are more vibrant than I've ever seen them, sparkling purple with flecks of gold mirroring the luxurious room. My silver hair flows around my shoulders, shining as if a light has been ignited inside me, illuminating this moment of strangeness.

"It's just the lighting," I tell myself, but deep down, I know it's something more. The transformation is undeniable. There's a newfound energy coursing through me, a reflection of the bond I've formed with Wilder.

I trace the outline of his primal claim that he left on my neck with my fingertips, marveling at the sensation that shoots through me. It feels as if finding my fated mate has unlocked a part of me I never knew existed, a promise of warmth and acceptance that feels foreign but intoxicating. It's exhilarating, the way he makes me feel.

I take a deep breath and glance around the rest of the bathroom, feeling the need to distract myself from the weight of possibility that comes with being bound to someone like him. My eyes land on an extravagant shower with a touch-screen panel. I can't help but admire the sleek design, the way it curves invitingly, beckoning me.

I press a few buttons, and the hot shower springs to life, steam rising as I stand there, a witness to its magic. Deciding a shower sounds good, I slip inside, and the warmth envelops me instantly. It feels like a holy experience.

Shower heads spray water from different directions, the sensation hitting my skin from all angles, like a gentle embrace. I close my eyes, surrendering to the warmth, letting it wash away the remnants of my past and the fatigue clinging to my muscles.

"Incredible, isn't it?" Wilder's voice pulls me from my reverie, and I open my eyes to find him standing just outside the glass doors, a playful smile on his lips.

The air shifts.

The chill from the bathroom slips in through the gap, mingling with the steamy warmth of the shower. My heart quickens as I register the sight of him, drenched in an aura of confidence that complements his striking features.

"Mind if I join you?" he asks, raising an eyebrow, his gaze unwavering.

I step back slightly, allowing him access. "I, uh … I wouldn't mind."

He doesn't need any further permission. Wilder steps inside, water cascading over his sculpted chest, glistening in a dazzling display. The contrast of hot water against his skin is mesmerizing. He catches my eye, and the corners of his mouth curl upward, satisfied as he meets my gaze.

"You look beautiful like this," he murmurs, taking a step closer, the warmth radiating between us as the water continues to drench our bodies.

A flutter of heat rushes through me at his compliment. I feel my cheeks flush, the water a fitting backdrop for the vulnerability pooling between us.

"What does this all mean?" I ask, voice a bit shaky.

He steps closer, grasping my hips and pulling me against his hard chest, stealing my breath.

"It means you're finally awakening to who you really are, and this connection between us…" he trails off, leaning in just enough for his breath to mingle with the steam and send shivers down my spine.

Before I can comprehend his intent, he scoops me up into his arms. I gasp in surprise as he presses my back against the cool glass wall of the shower. "Wilder! You're going to drop me! I'm hea—" His deep growl echoes in the spacious room, the sound vibrating through the air, making my words die on my tongue. My heart races, pounding against my rib cage as panic and exhilaration wash over me.

His grip is firm yet gentle, as if he can feel the flutter of my insecurities but chooses to ignore them. "Relax," he whispers, his voice a low murmur, laced with an intensity that sends heat pooling deep within me.

In that moment, I am not just the girl with doubts and fears, I am the girl who dares to succumb to the wildness within. My breath hitches as he leans closer, his warm breath teasing my lips, every fiber of my being resonating with the primal need pulsing in the space between us.

Just as I muster the courage to snap back to

reason, his lips capture mine. The kiss ignites everything inside me, an explosion that scatters my thoughts like leaves in a tempest. He tastes of sweetness and spice—a dangerous mix that has my senses reeling.

I watch as droplets of water cascade down Wilder's chiseled chest, the muscles rippling with each movement he makes. With each caress, he deepens the kiss, coaxing me to melt into him. My body responds instinctively, aligning with his in a rhythm both familiar and thrillingly new. The sensation of him pressed so intimately against me chases away any lingering chill, leaving only heat coursing through my veins.

Wilder's lips trail from my mouth along my jawline, a skilled explorer charting the rise and fall of my breaths. Each touch ignites fires across my skin, culminating with his tongue's bold sweep over the sensitive mark he left on my neck. I gasp, an involuntary sound of delight and bewilderment, feeling those waves of pleasure surge from the point of contact like ripples across a pond.

Wilder…" I sigh, barely managing to keep my eyes trained on his, the shock of my previous rationality melting into a raw and primal hunger.

"Shhh," he teases softly, his breath warm against my ear.

"I've got you." His strong body presses against mine, his hard length tantalizingly close to my entrance. A deep, insatiable need unfurls within me at the connection, an urgent longing to be fully enveloped by him.

He grips my ass hard in one hand then guides his thick cock to my pussy, circling my clit.

"Mmm, so wet for me. Who does this cunt drip for?" he growls against my ear, sending goose bumps along my fevered skin. His eyes darken with desire, a promise that makes me tingle. I clench my eyes shut, overwhelmed by his raw desire, as I respond with a whimper, unable to deny the truth of his words.

With a swift motion, he plunges his fingers deep inside me, igniting a blazing trail of pleasure that courses through my veins. Each thrust is precise, powerful, sending waves of ecstasy crashing through me. My legs tremble, but Wilder's strong arm holds me up, keeping me firmly pressed against the cool glass of the shower wall, my body stripped bare of defenses.

Suddenly, his fingers withdraw, leaving me aching, gasping for more. "No, don't…" I protest, almost desperately, but he swiftly drops me and spins me around.

"You want it, don't you?" he snarls, that raw hunger evident in every word. His hard cock presses against my ass, pulsating with need. I can feel the heat radiating off him, the proof of his desire. His hand snakes around my waist once again, finding my clit, igniting the maddening rhythm that leaves me moaning with need.

"Beg for it, Arwen," he commands, his breath hot against my ear. "Beg for my cock."

His demand sends my mind reeling, caught in the storm of need that clouds my judgment. "Please, Wilder … I need you inside me." The plea escapes my lips, raw and desperate.

With a throaty growl, Wilder positions himself at my entrance, teasing my slick folds with the head of his cock. I feel like I am on the brink of something monumental, something beyond mere pleasure. Without warning, he thrusts into me, filling me to the hilt with one powerful movement. The sensation sends shock waves through every nerve ending, the mixture of pleasure and pain almost too much to bear. An animalistic cry escapes my lips, echoing in the steam-filled room as he sets a brutal pace, his powerful thrusts forcing my sensitive nipples to rub against the cool glass.

"You didn't answer me, Starlight," he urges, grinding against me, making it impossible to think clearly. "Who makes this pussy so slick with need?"

"Wilder! It's only you," I cry out, overwhelmed by need and the way he is manipulating my body as if it's an instrument.

"Fuck, Arwen…" he groans, the sound reverberating in my core. "You feel so good. So fucking tight."

"Tell me you want it, tell me you need it!" Wilder demands, his voice a harsh whisper in the haze of steam.

I can barely form the words, overcome by the onslaught of pleasure that consumes me. "Please, Wilder … I can't hold back!" My body responds to him, arching and grinding against him, every instinct screaming for release.

With every thrust, I feel the tension build within me, the waves of pleasure crashing harder and harder, threatening to pull me under with its sheer force. I can hear my heartbeat thundering in my ears, the sound almost drowned out by Wilder's own growls as he surrenders to the rhythm of our bodies colliding.

"Just surrender, Starlight. I'll take you to places you've never been," he promises.

My body tightens around him, clenching as I teeter at the edge of ecstasy.

"Wilder!" I scream, the pleasure crashing over me like a relentless wave, dragging me down into oblivion. With each powerful thrust, he pushes me further into bliss, our world spinning out of control as we surrender to the tempest of our desires.

He pumps one last time, gripping me tightly, his cock twitching deep inside me as he empties himself into me. A moan escapes my lips, swallowed by the cascading water. We stand there, panting and spent, surrendering to the bliss that washes over us, both physical and emotional.

Wilder presses a gentle kiss to my shoulder, a stark contrast to the rough, animalistic way he just took me.

"You're mine, Arwen," he murmurs against my skin as his arms wrap tightly around me. The possessiveness in his voice both thrills and soothes my frayed nerves.

He delivers a playful slap to my ass, sending a fresh wave of pleasure coursing through me. It is an electric jolt, a reminder of his control, followed swiftly by his hands working to ease the sting. Then, with a swift movement, he twists me around, cupping my face in his hands.

"And you're mine." A wicked glimmer sparks in Wilder's eyes.

"My sweet, delicious mate," he muses as he brings his lips to mine, kissing me with such reverence and love it leaves me breathless. *Can he truly love my shattered soul?*

As if reading my thoughts, he broke the kiss but kept my gaze locked on his.

"Let's wash up. I have a surprise for you," he says with a smirk, lathering a cloth with his soap. Heat surges through me anew as his strong hands begin at my chest, lingering for a tantalizing moment over my breast. A mischievous grin spreads across his face.

"Wilder…" my voice falters, breathy and unwilling to sound firm. I am caught in the web of my conflicting emotions and desires.

He chuckles darkly, eyes dancing with mischief. "Yes?" His smile is devious, his playful intentions clear.

"I thought we needed to get clean?" I challenge, raising an eyebrow as the water cascades around us, doing little to douse the fire in my belly.

"I take that responsibility very seriously, Starlight," he jokes, laughter rumbling from deep within him. That sound, rich and vibrant, fills the cavernous space and brings warmth, pushing aside the remnants of doubt that cling to my heart. My happiness bubbles up, brightening the heavy atmosphere that had previously burdened me.

"Maybe I should finish so you don't run all the hot water out with how … precise you are," I retort, matching his grin with one of my own.

"On second thought, I want my cum dripping from you so everyone can smell me on you." The words roll off his tongue like a dark promise. He taps a button behind me, and suddenly, the jets cease, silence cutting through our postcoital haze.

"Hey!" I yelp, shocked and somewhat outraged.

"You were right. We have somewhere to be," he beams down, pulling me from the shower and wrapping me in a heated towel as if he conjured it from thin air. His attention to detail is maddeningly impressive and makes my heart race even faster.

I blink up at him, my hair dripping and messy, but I don't care. The intensity in his gaze, the way he holds me close, makes me forget everything outside of this moment.

"What's the surprise?" I whisper, my curiosity piqued as he leads me out of the steamy sanctuary and into the coolness of his room.

Wilder grins, a playful glint in his eyes, making me wonder what he has planned. I'm about to find out just what surprises are in store for the day.

Chapter Seven

Wilder

After Kody and I spoke, I called in a favor with a boutique close to my place. The owner owed me more than a few after-dark dealings over the years, and I seized the opportunity to pamper Arwen, my sweet little mate. I want her to have the best of everything, starting with a brand-new wardrobe. The items were delivered while we were in the shower, allowing me to lead her straight to her large walk-in closet. This isn't the surprise I was referring to but it's a start.

"What is all this?" Arwen gasps, freezing in my arms. Her eyes roam over the filled shelves, a mix of astonishment and confusion painting her features. I lean down, pressing my lips to her neck, letting the warmth of my breath soothe her.

"I got you a few new things."

"A few? This is a whole store, Wilder! I don't need all this." She spins around, her long, wet hair slapping me in the chest, a mini tidal wave of silk falling as if teasing me.

"Choose something. I'm taking you out tonight." I feel excitement burst beneath my skin like a fire igniting. Taking her out is a mission I have planned well beyond a simple dinner.

Her eyes widen, luminous and full of enchantment, and she turns back to the closet, the choices now all tantalizingly laid out before her. She runs her hands over the different materials, delicate silks and glimmering sequins, until she stops at a short black lace dress. The way it clings and drapes over the hanger makes my breath hitch.

She looks over her shoulder, biting her lip, and that sight alone has my cock ready for her again. A gasp escapes my mouth as her innocent demeanor ignites a lust deep within. I don't think there will come a time when I don't want to be inside the heaven between her legs.

"How's this one?" Her voice is playful, eyes sparkling mischievously as she bats her eyelashes at me. I am powerless to say no, even as a dark part of my mind simmers with protectiveness at the thought of other eyes devouring her in that dress.

"It's perfect." I approve, leaning casually against the doorframe, trying not to reveal the turmoil inside me.

Arwen spins back to the collection of shoes I picked, heels that seem to amplify her every movement. "I can't believe you did all this." Her soft voice holds astonishment, her disbelief apparent as she lifts a delicate stiletto and examines it like a curious child with an enchanting toy.

Surely, she can believe I would do anything for her. In the grand scheme of our lives, buying clothes feels minuscule. But as I look back, the image of her in that depressing apartment comes flooding back. The anger coils within me like a serpent striking at the injustice of it all. She should've never lived like that—alone, with walls that didn't love her back.

"You deserve all of this and so much more, Arwen." I finally say, stepping beside her, my voice low with sincerity. "I want to keep you safe, and I want to see you shine."

She turns to me, her eyes glistening with a mix of gratitude and something deeper, something that draws me in. "Wilder, you're more than I ever thought I'd find. It's like—" She hesitates, deep in thought. "You make me feel whole."

The words hang in the air like a spell, casting a

soft warmth over my hardened heart. I reach to pull her closer, feeling her body pressed against mine, and I lose myself in the gaze of those brilliant violet eyes. She might as well be my soul, the woven essence of magic entwined with humanity.

With a mischievous glint in her eye, Arwen tugs on the black lace dress and holds it up, inspecting herself in the full-length mirror inside the closet. "How do I look?"

"Just as I imagined," I say, stepping behind her, my breath ghosting over her shoulder again. "Like a goddess."

She blushes, the color adorning her cheeks like fresh rose blooms, stoking the flames of my desire.

"So, where are we going?" she asks, turning slightly, her fingers brushing against mine, their softness igniting an urge to keep her close.

"You'll have to wait and see." I smile, pulling her in close and loving my scent coming from her. Everyone at The Gin Room will smell her and know she's mine, completely and utterly mine.

****

The night pulses with energy as I rev the engine of my gunmetal gray McLaren 5S07. My nights typically begin with the rumble of my bike beneath me, but tonight is different. Tonight, luxury and comfort take precedence, and I'm more than happy to share the exhilarating ride with a vision of ethereal beauty sitting beside me.

Arwen. Her name rolls off the tongue like a whisper of silk—a name that should be stitched into the very stars above. As I urge the accelerator deeper, her laughter slices through the air, suspended in the moment as the cool breeze tousles her silver strands, like long-lost memories caught in a dance with the night. I glance sideways, catching the ghostly reflection of the moonlight glimmering on the tops of her thighs, barely constrained by the delicate fabric of her lace dress. They seem to glow, calling to me, a siren song weaving its treacherous route deep into my thoughts.

"Faster!" she teases, her voice melodic, threaded with mischief.

With her command, I push the pedal harder, the McLaren responding with a vicious growl, transforming the city into a blur of lights and shadows. Each street we pass resonates with whispers of the unknown, merging the mundane with the magical. The neon signs flicker like dying stars, and in that moment, it feels as if the fabric of reality is flickering with us, embracing our wild abandon.

But my focus remains tethered to Arwen. She's captivating—a radiant enchantress crafted from moonbeams and dreams. As her head leans back against the plush leather seat, I catch a glimpse of her full lips, curved in a playful smile that threatens to unravel my resolve. I can almost feel her essence, ethereal yet tangible—a guardian of the night who ought not to be veiled by the chaos of the streets.

We reach a quiet stretch of road, the city fading behind us like an unwanted past. My puma surges with a primal energy that demands recklessness. Without thought, I swerve to pull the car to a halt, tires screeching slightly, the remnants of city life disappearing in the breath of a heartbeat.

"What are you doing?" Arwen asks.

"Arwen..." I murmur, the name escaping my lips like sacrilege, like a prayer laced with desire. "Come here."

Her eyes sparkle, the kind that make a man ache to be close, to be enveloped in the ecstasies of life unchained. My heart thunders against my chest as I turn to her, every muscle straining against a world filled with rules and restraint. With a flick of her wrist, she undoes the seat belt, a daring invitation sparking in the space between us.

I slide across the warm leather, the distance evaporating into a soft sigh, as her intoxicating scent washes over me. Grabbing her hips, I swing her around to straddle my waist. All logic fractures as I press my lips against hers, a collision of fire and ice. Just as her mouth opens to me, I feel every ounce of sanity dissolve into the electric air around us.

The world becomes a cacophony of thrilling sensations, her body molding against mine like a perfect tapestry of need. The moon hangs above us, complicit in our desires, its silvery glow bathing us in an otherworldly light. As I push my hands against the curvature of her thighs, grasping that heavenly skin, my body ignites with primal urgency—a hunger that cannot be quelled.

"Reckless, isn't it?" she whispers, a teasing challenge sparkling in her gaze. Her fingers grip my shirt, playful yet possessive.

"Just a little..." I murmur against her lips.

"Wilder..." she breathes, biting her lip. My pulse races at the sound of my name in her mouth, wrapped in desire. Her hips begin rocking against my hard length, eliciting a groan from me. "I need you."

"Is my girl wet?" I wonder aloud, fingers gliding up to follow the trail of heat that radiates from her core to where I can feel her soft warmth through the fabric. The way she quivers beneath my touch compels me forward, a thief in the night reaching for a treasure. Her teeth bite into her plump bottom lip as she grins, a seductive invitation.

"Gods, you're naughty," I tease, the words slipping from my lips like sweet nectar. I pull aside her delicate thong, my fingers craving the heat radiating from her core, sliding onto that soft warmth.

"Wilder!" she gasps as I slip between her slick folds, and I grunt in response, feeling her excitement surge.

"Fuck, you're soaked." My voice is low, gruff with need.

"I'm going to pump you so full of my cum that it's dripping down this perfect cunt, so everyone can see and smell who you belong to," I breathe into the shell of her ear, the heat of my words merging with the heat radiating from her core. Her breath catches, a gasp escaping her lips, giving me all the encouragement I need.

"Take me out," I demand, shoving her back slightly before guiding her hands toward my zipper. Her small hand palms my throbbing length, teasingly drawing back and forth over the fabric. Arwen's small hand palms my throbbing cock before she releases it. My resolve wobbles, and I waste no time pulling her closer. With one swift motion, I thrust into her, engulfing myself entirely in her warmth, the precarious moment of pure possession crashing like a tidal wave against our skin.

It's fast, rough—a primal claim. Each pump sends pleasure rippling through me as she clenches around my shaft, her release building.

"Fuck, Wilder," she moans, her nails digging into my shoulders, pushing down to meet each frantic thrust.

"That's it, baby, take my dick. You're mine, and I'm never letting you go," I promise. I can feel my own orgasm building, my balls tightening as I pound into her.

"Wilder, it's too much, I—"

"Don't hold back! Let go!" I urge, tracing quick circles against her sensitive clit. My body moves with a desperate rhythm, pushing closer to euphoria, and the soft gasps slipping from her mouth urge me on. Then I feel her tightness increasing, the waves of her climax thrumming between us.

"Yes! Yes!" she whimpers, her legs tightening around me.

With a ferocious thrust, I empty myself inside her, a cataclysmic explosion that feels like eternity. My heart races as I physically feel her tense around me, milking every drop I've devoted to her.

"Mine," I growl, as she collapses on my chest, her breath cooling my skin. "Now clench that pussy and keep my cum where it belongs," I demand, sitting her back on the seat. I lean over her and pull the seat belt to secure it myself. Her eyes sparkle even in the low light, a glimmer filled with mischief and submission.

"Where to?" she asks.

"The Gin Room." I shift into gear, eager to share this part of me with her.

****

Arwen

We come to a stop in front of a large, sophisticated bar. Glimmers of vibrant light dance in the reflections on the polished surface of the building, hints of the extravagance within. I've never really ventured to this side of the city; I was always one to keep to the darkened corners of Manhattan, the places where shadows hold secrets and whispers carry the weight of unspoken pasts.

Looking down at my dress, the black lace seems to wrap around me like a spell. I smooth any wrinkles out of the fabric, suddenly feeling insecure about my appearance. I can't shake the thought that I might as well have "poor" stamped across my face. I feel utterly out of place among the vibrant elegance of the city's elite. And then there's Wilder.

Wilder leans back casually in the car seat, his dark

hair perfectly tousled, his wealthy aura wrapping around him like an expensive cologne. It's enough to make my stomach churn. He jumps from the car, tossing his keys to the valet as though they possess no worth to him, before coming over to my side of the car and opening the door.

"Come on, Starlight. I want to show you off," he purrs into my ear, and my heart skips, an erratic beat I try to harness as I grasp his hand. The heat pooling within me is only partially embarrassment, it's more than the fact that his touch holds power. He pulls me close, and I can feel the heat radiating from his body. But another heat lingers, a reminder of the wild night we had only moments ago.

My body betrays me as I realize just how much I'm being affected, feeling the remnants of our intimacy shift uncomfortably between my thighs. My cheeks flame with heat, and I press my legs closer together in a futile attempt to maintain some semblance of decorum while navigating the precarious high heels he insisted I wear. His grip on my hand tightens as he leads me toward the double glass doors that loom ahead.

"Welcome, Mr. Black," the doorman intones, bowing his head and pulling the handle back with an elegant flourish. Wilder smiles, the corners of his lips curling up, but it feels predatory, as if he knows more than he lets on. I steal a glance at him, confusion swirling in my mind. I barely know this man and he's supposed to be my mate but I can't help feeling inferior.

Before I can dwell, the room opens up into a lavish spectacle of luxury the likes of which I've only seen in movies—the bright gleam of crystal chandeliers, dimmed shades of wine-red velvet, and the soft hum of hushed conversations blend seamlessly with the gentle clinking of glasses.

Standing on the brink of this new world, I

suddenly feel small and delicate, like a flower straining against the winds of uncertainty. With this kind of opulence at his fingertips, *why did he wander into my bar?* Alley Katz is a shithole by comparison.

"Would you like a drink?" he whispers, leaning closer as he guides me to a plush booth on the side of the room. The velvet of the seating envelops me luxuriously, but as I sit back, unease settles into my stomach. It dawns on me that I'll probably leave behind a mess from our earlier escapade. Just when I think I might shrink into my seat, he turns his full attention on me.

"Um … sure," I manage, my voice barely a whisper. I bite my lip, trying desperately to avoid his intense yellow eyes, so fiery yet so unreadable.

Wilder flicks his wrist in an elegant motion, and in an instant, there is a server before us, appearing almost as if he had materialized from thin air.

"Good evening." The man bows deeply. "The usual, Mr. Black?" Wilder merely nods, his attention still riveted on me.

"And for you, Miss?" he asks as his eyes rake over my exposed flesh. Before I can respond, before I can think, Wilder's arm snaps out, grabbing the server by the throat, hoisting him effortlessly from the ground. My heart plummets into my stomach, horror spilling into every corner of my being.

"Don't. You. Dare. Look. At. Her," he hisses, enunciating each word with a cold precision that leaves me shocked. The server's face pales, panic clear in his expression. A squeak escapes him, followed by a whisper of a "yes, sir," before Wilder unceremoniously drops him back onto the floor.

Wilder's eyes are wild, feral in their intensity as they meet mine. Instinctively I lean back, curling inward, feeling the fear coursing through me like ice water. He straightens his suit, smoothing down the fabric as if he hadn't just threatened the life of a mere waiter. Then he slips back into the booth, all too casual, as if the tempest he'd just unleashed was beneath him.

An alternate gentleman, somewhat frazzled, scurries over, sidestepping the quivering server lying on the floor.

"I apologize, Mr. Black. I will get your order right away. Macallan, neat, and..." He doesn't dare look at me, his eyes remain on Wilder's.

"The Club Gin Fizz," he orders without even asking what I prefer. Wilder's order hangs in the air, and anger bristles in my stomach at being treated like a child unable to make her own decisions.

"I could have ordered for myself!" I exclaim, flaring my nostrils as my heart pounds in righteous offense. Wilder chuckles smoothly, tilting his head slightly, giving me that devilish grin that both irritates and mystifies me.

"Let me treat you to something new."

"But you don't even know what I like!" I counter, but it's half-hearted, as the flames from the previous intense scene make me feel flustered.

"Perhaps one sip of this Club Gin Fizz, and I will learn forever what you adore," he declares, though there's that dangerous glint in his eyes again, a promise of fervor coated in mystery. I'm caught, suddenly fascinated, yet in a whirlwind of emotion—dread, fear, and budding intrigue entwining themselves around my heart.

Before long, the server returns, eyes still averted, placing our drinks delicately on the table between us. As the world spins and sways in the intoxicating atmosphere of The Gin Room, I can't shake the feeling that tonight, my life is about to spiral into a darkness that makes my past look like a mere shadow.

Wilder clinks his glass against mine, a spark of excitement dancing in his eyes as he tips back his drink. I watch him, unable to ignore the sense of anticipation laced with dread that coils in my gut.

After a few drinks, Wilder checks his watch, the glint of the crystal catching my eye like some unspoken omen. "It's time," he announces, finishing the remnants of his expensive whiskey in one swift motion. Confusion swirls through my mind. I thought this was the surprise he was talking about.

"What—" I start, but I'm interrupted.

"There's my boy." A tall, muscular man strides in, his presence commanding and vibrant. His grin spreads like wildfire as he locks eyes with Wilder. He jumps from his seat, buttoning his jacket before he slaps the man on the back. Clearly these two are close and a pang of jealousy washes over me. I wish I had a friend. I guess Kit is the closest thing I had to a friend, and who knows if I'll ever see her again.

"Kody, this is Arwen," Wilder introduces, grabbing my hand and pulling me from the booth with a force that almost sends me sprawling. My body wobbles on the unforgiving stiletto heels. I instinctively reach my hand toward Kody for a formal greeting, but it's abruptly seized and tucked against my side, like I'm some delicate artifact rather than a person. Kody laughs, the sound rich and velvety, but it only ignites the flame of my irritation.

"It's nice to meet you, Arwen," he replies with an exaggerated little bow, as if I'm the Queen of England herself. "So, are you ready?" Kody's glance drifts toward Wilder, his question amplifying my confusion, sparking a litany of questions that race through my mind. Catching Wilder's eye, I shoot him a questioning glance. There's an undercurrent to this moment I'm not privy to. *What does he mean by 'ready'?*

Wilder, oblivious to my mounting unease, replies casually, "We were just about to head down there." A note of excitement echoes in his voice.

"Down where?" I find my voice, but none of them acknowledge me as Wilder pulls me closer to his side. Instead of leading me out of the bar, we veer down a long, dim corridor that is lined with shadows that seem to breathe. An eerie feeling settles over me, each step amplifying the disquieting atmosphere, my heart racing faster with uncertainty.

"So, is this part of your surprise?" I ask, forcing a light tone. My voice sounds hollow against the nighttime stillness that envelops us. Wilder turns his face toward me, and beneath the edges of the harsh lighting, I see an eagerness that masks something darker, something ominous.

As we reach a door at the end of the dimly lit corridor, Kody pauses, pulling it open with a drama that would rival the grandest theatrical performance. The air inside is thick with the stench of sweat, adrenaline, and a metallic tang of iron—like the taste of blood that lingers at the back of my throat. Wilder stands beside me, seemingly oblivious to my distress, as if this subterranean world is a casual Saturday night affair for him. His smile is unnervingly bright, each tooth gleaming under the flickering, antiquated lamps, while I feel a suffocating panic creeping into my bones, threatening to paralyze me.

"Welcome to the Shifter Fight Club," Wilder leans down to shout over the roar of the crowd.

A fight club?

That's what he wanted to bring me to?

What in the world possessed him to think I would be interested in something like this?

He knows what I've been through, saw it firsthand, and now he's thrusting me into a world filled with men likely even more aggressive than my ex.

My heart pounds against my rib cage as I take in the sight before me: muscular shifters, dripping with sweat, circling each other like predators, their claws and faces smeared with blood and grime. The crowd's cheers and jeers blend into a deafening cacophony that vibrates through the concrete walls. The atmosphere is charged with a primal energy that makes my skin crawl. I can feel my pulse hammering in my ears, each beat a reminder of my escalating fear.

A mix of fear, anger, and betrayal courses through my body. I am ready to bolt back up the stairs, get as far away from this nightmare as possible. My breathing becomes shallow, my hands trembling as I clutch my bag to my chest. I feel the walls closing in, the air too thick to breathe, my vision narrowing to a tunnel as the panic sets in.

And through it all, Wilder's smile never falters, as if this is exactly where he belongs, while I am left to wonder how I will ever escape this hellish place. *Are we truly meant to be together?*

"Is this your idea of a good time?" I ask, my tone an unfamiliar mix of incredulity and fright. My heartbeat thunders in my ears, so loud it drowns out the chaos around us.

"It's amazing!" he shouts, squeezing my shoulder as if trying to share his enthusiasm through sheer physical presence. "You'll love it!"

But love is the last thing I feel. I scan the crowd, taking in the rough faces contorted with intensity. Their shouts of encouragement and displeasure blend into a singular roar that echoes off the brick walls. In the center of the room, two figures are locked in combat, muscles rippling, claws and tails swinging. These are not just spry men, but shifters—creatures who embody the spirit of beasts. Muscles ripple like waves beneath their skin, and when their bodies make contact, the force reverberates through the floor like the crash of thunder.

My heart hammers in my chest, my breathing shallow and rapid. The stench of sweat, blood, and adrenaline fills the air, and I can taste the metallic tang of iron at the back of my throat. Panic grips me, tightening my chest and making my vision blur around the edges. I feel as if I am being crushed by the weight of the oppressive atmosphere, the crowd's energy suffocating me.

"Wilder," I whisper, my voice barely audible over the din. "I can't be here. I need to leave."

He looks at me, his eyes gleaming with excitement and a hint of mischief. "Trust me," he says, plopping a kiss on top of my head. "You'll get used to it." When he sees the look of panic in my eyes, I think he's about to tell me we can leave.

Wilder leans closer, his breath warm against my ear. "You'll see. It's liberating!" His eyes sparkle with a fervor I have never seen before, drawing me into a vortex of confusion.

"Come on, man. We need to get you signed in," Kody chimes in beside us. *Wait? What the actual fuck?* Realization dawns, crashing through my stupor—a planetary alignment of horror unrolls in slow motion before me.

"Y-you're fighting?" The words slip from my mouth in disbelief. Surely I misheard him, this has to be some elaborate prank. Wilder, the vibrant and charming face of my sanity, is about to stand in that very ring.

His features light up at my question, the spark in his eyes captivating yet infuriating. "Of course! And you'll get to see me shift." He winks.

"Wilder, this is reckless! You're going to get

hurt!" The words tumble frantically from my lips without consideration for decorum, emotions shattering like glass with each syllable.

"He's undefeated," Kody booms as people turn to look at us. Suddenly, Wilder is swallowed up in a sea of people, all chanting his name.

"Black! Black!"

Panic surges through me as I watch Wilder disappear into the throng. My heart races, and my breaths come in shallow gasps. The crowd's energy is overwhelming, their excitement a stark contrast to my mounting fear. I feel a crushing weight on my chest, the oppressive atmosphere closing in around me.

The roar of the crowd grows louder, their chants echoing off the brick walls. I can barely hear my own thoughts over the deafening noise. The sight of Wilder, my anchor in this chaotic world, being swept away fills me with a sense of helplessness. I want to reach out, to pull him back, but my feet feel rooted to the spot.

Where am I?

How have I stumbled into this mad vortex?

A cold dread washes over me, my stomach twisting into knots. Watching Wilder shift and fight in that pit of chaos fills me with a sense of impending doom. The thought of seeing my mate transform into a beast and engage in violent combat is too much to bear. Memories of past traumas flood my mind, each one a sharp reminder of the pain and fear I've endured. My heart races, my breaths coming in shallow, rapid gasps.

I'm seated with Kody as my mandatory guardian, as Wilder put it, while he gets into the ring. He forbade me to leave his side like I'm a petulant child. I don't know whether to laugh or cry at his audacity to stick me with a babysitter. I've been on my own most of my life, I'm not as fragile like glass.

Just then, Wilder emerges from the dressing room, his athletic physique a charming shock of sinew and strength beneath the blaring spotlight. The crowd erupts into a roar, drowning out my thoughts. My attention zeroes in on him as if he were the sun, and I a mere moth drawn to his glow.

But I'm not the only one drawn to Wilder's brilliant flame. A striking woman, with hair cascading like a waterfall of shimmering obsidian, approaches him, her smile syrupy sweet. My stomach twists, a furious tempest gathering as she trails her finger across his arm, the very act laced with a familiarity that ignites a spark of rage in me.

Wilder's head snaps my way, his piercing yellow eyes locking onto mine with an intensity that sends shivers racing down my spine. Somewhere, deep within the unyielding steel of his gaze, his expression turns inscrutable, but I'm certain he felt my anger. I want to run to him, to scream at him to remember who I am.

A laugh erupts from the crowd, pulling me out of my brooding thoughts, and I close my eyes tightly against the noise, willing myself to drown in silence. I attempt to hum softly, but all I can hear is chaos—the pounding of feet, the shouts of the spectators, the bass of the announcer's booming voice amplifying the turmoil inside me.

"Wilder Black is back for another round!" the announcer bellows through the speakers. A deafening roar erupts from the crowd, vibrating through me, causing my heart to race. With a pang of reluctance, I crack open my eyes to the spectacle before me. Wilder stands at one corner of the ring, muscles taut and ready, a fierce glare etched onto his face.

First impressions could shatter illusions, and in this case, this man was all foreboding menace. His form radiates raw energy—a shadow that swallows the light around him, his golden hair a stark contrast that shimmers like spun gold against the darkness of the venue. However, it is his eyes—amber, encircled in an unholy red—that sends a chilling shiver weaving through my very bones. Staring into those depths feels akin to gazing into the abyss, where darkness thrives.

The announcer's voice echoes again, full of raw excitement, letting loose the story behind this deadly showdown. "Jasper Quinton placed a bet with Wilder that he couldn't ignore, which brings us here tonight!" He moves the microphone away briefly to exchange some inaudible words with the two men. Judging by Wilder's grimace, I can only imagine it's a taunt, one that is stoking the fire, igniting the fight.

"This is another fight to the death. The only way out of this ring is if either opponent is dead," he yells, hyping the audience into a fevered frenzy. The crowd rises in unison, a wild storm of bodies, their anticipation crackling in the air like a thunderstorm on the verge of breaking. I'm pushed and shoved as people try to get a better view of the arena. Kody pulls me back just in time before I faceplant into the row below us.

"And now, without further ado … shift!" The announcer's hand slams down on the bell, piercing the charged atmosphere. I watch, breathless, as Wilder begins his transformation. It is beautifully horrific, a chaotic ballet of sinew and bone. I feel sick as the sounds of bones cracking and reshaping echo in my ears. I grew up amongst humans, had only read about shifters in whispered tales, and now witnessing it unfurl is both majestic and terrifying. With a final snap and twist, Wilder's form morphs into a black puma. His fur glistens, absorbing the light and giving way to the darkness. The shifter leaps into the air with a lithe elegance, his landing a resonant thud that sends tremors through the ground, urging the spectators into a hysteria of chanting his name. "Wilder! Wilder!"

A flurry of movement catches my attention—a blur in my peripheral vision. I turn just in time to catch a glimpse of Jasper, who is shifting as well. Wings flash, enormous and feathered, a resplendent display of power. My breath hitching in my throat, I realize that Jasper is morphing into some kind of beast, a creature not of this world.

"What is he?" I gasp to Kody.

"He's a griffin, a rare mystical breed. Capable of aerial and ground assaults," he mutters, his expression grave.

The two beasts circle one another, the puma's grace a sharp contrast to the griffin's raw might. I can feel the air quake with their unrelenting intent. Wilder prowls forward, a fluid shadow, muscles coiling as he positions himself for a strike.

And then, all at once, the battlefield explodes into mayhem. The puma lunges, vaulting with astonishing agility, narrowly escaping the crushing grasp of the griffin.

Kody leans into me to whisper, "Jasper called this fight for revenge against his fallen friend, Draken. Wilder will never say no to a challenge." The words send a quiver down my spine, as dread pools in my gut like lead. I can feel the sick, intoxicating hunger for blood pulsating from Wilder, and it claws at my insides. Our mated bond ignites, forcing his emotions into my very being— darkness, rage, bloodlust. I don't want to witness this. I have seen enough violence to last a lifetime.

With a flash of pure instinct, Wilder lashes out, claws aimed for the area exposed as Jasper flaps his wings. The arena echoes with primal roars and tortured cries as neither will relent. The clock is ticking, and though onlookers writhe in cruel anticipation, I know this isn't merely a fight, it is a battle of wills, a clash of destiny and power, with everything at stake.

A voice nearby yells, "He can harness the power of the winds—it's a deadly combination when you're allowed to soar. Wilder needs to stay grounded!" My feet feel glued to the earth, paralyzed by the horror unfolding before me, but every instinct in my body screams for me to escape.

I have to run.

Without a second thought, I bolt, weaving through throngs of spectators each eager for blood, despair coursing through me. I shove my way through the nightmare of bodies, driven by an intrinsic need to escape. To be anywhere but here, a world of chaos and pain. Each shove and push only deepens the urgency in my heart as I hear a sickening clash behind me, a collision of bodies. *Crack!* Bones breaking, bodies tearing. I stumble, tears streaming down my cheeks, blurring my vision, but the instinct to get away propels me forward.

As I near the exit, pushing past the jostling crowd, my heart shatters with each anguished cry that echoes behind me, a reminder of the blood-soaked reality that my mate is fighting for his life in a ring of savage violence.

"No! I can't do this!" I cry, my breaths ragged, as I burst free into the cool night air. With every ounce of will, I flee the desolate arena, desperate to leave behind the slaughter. Though I know as a shifter's mate, I'll never fully escape the darkness that comes with our bond, entwined with the violence of their world.

The fresh air hits me like a wave, but it does little to calm the storm raging inside. My legs give out, and I collapse onto the ground, my body trembling uncontrollably. The world around me blurs as my vision narrows, and I can feel the walls of panic closing in. My breaths come in short, shallow gasps, each one a struggle against the suffocating weight pressing down on my chest.

I clutch at the ground, my fingers digging into the concrete as if it could anchor me to reality. The sounds of the fight club still echo in my ears, a haunting reminder of the madness I've just escaped. My heart races, pounding against my rib cage like a trapped bird desperate to break free. Tears stream down my face, hot and unrelenting, as I fight to regain control.

But the panic is relentless, a tidal wave of fear and helplessness that threatens to drown me. I curl into myself, trying to make myself as small as possible, as if I could disappear from the world and the horrors it holds. My mind races, thoughts tumbling over each other in a jumbled frenzy. The image of Wilder, fighting and shifting, is burned into my mind, a constant source of terror.

I don't know how long I laid there, lost in the grip of my panic attack. Minutes feel like hours, each second stretching into an eternity. Slowly, painfully, I force myself to take deeper breaths, to focus on the sensation of the cool air filling my lungs. Gradually, the tightness in my chest begins to ease, and the world starts to come back into focus.

I look left and right, wondering where to go. I'm basically homeless unless I call Wilder's place my home, and right now, I'm not sure that I do. I throw my hand in the air, intending to flag down a passing taxi when pain suddenly radiates through my head. The next thing I know, I'm falling into the darkness that awaits me.

Chapter Eight

Wilder

My puma crouches low, as my sleek black fur blends with the shadows, keeping my eyes locked on my opponent. Every move I take is with the grace and precision of a predator, my muscles taut with anticipation. The thrill of the fight barrels through me. The griffin stands in his corner, towering and majestic as he spreads his wings wide, the golden feathers catching in the flickering light. He screeches and lunges forward, talons extended, gleaming like knives.

I dodge to the side, narrowly avoiding the griffin's razor-sharp talons. I retaliate with a swift swipe of my own, claws slashing through the air. Jasper roars in pain as my claws find purchase, leaving deep gouges in his flank. The beast staggers back, eyes blazing with rage. I can feel the heat rising as he gains altitude, but I anticipated this. Timing is crucial. I unleash all my strength and spring upward, aiming to meet him mid-air. My powerful hind legs propel me like a missile, ready for our inevitable collision. We strike with a bone-jarring impact, feathers and fur mingling in a whirlwind of motion. My claws somehow find their way to his shoulder, sinking in deeply. Jasper lets out a roar, and the audience wails, the vivacity of the moment washing over me.

In our tangled fall to the ground, the scent of sweat and fear intermingle, a fragrant reminder of the stakes at play. I've never been beaten and I intend on staying that way. But the thought is fleeting. With every visceral struggle over dominance, a strange tingle lances through me.

Suddenly, a chill shoots straight to my core as fear envelops me, but it isn't my own. It is Arwen's—our connection unfolds, sharp and revealing. I had mistaken her anxious energy all evening for excitement, thinking it was for the thrill of the fight. *But now? Now it is sheer panic.* Briefly, in the chaos, all I can see is her silver hair, shimmering like ethereal moonlight, as she dashes between the sea of bodies, tears flowing freely down her flawless cheeks. My beast roars, unleashing a sound that vibrates through the cramped space, drowning out the cheers and jeers that mix together. Desperation drives the command, a primal urge to go to her. She is all that matters—not my fight, not this ring.

The precious moments I let my guard down became precisely the opening Jasper needed. He beat his wings together, creating a powerful gust of wind that throws me off balance and sends me tumbling to the ground, disoriented.

I curse at myself as I regain my footing. I can hear Jasper's throaty growl reverberating through the air above me, his shell of fury encasing him wholly. With a swift motion, he attempts to dive down upon me like a ravenous beast, his wings flapping with the might of a storm.

A surge of instinct floods my veins. I rush forward, using every ounce of strength in my sinewy muscles to leap out of his path. I feel the air whistle past me as his massive form hits the ground with a thud, missing me by mere inches.

I land gracefully on my feet, then turn instantly, watching Jasper's feet scramble to regain balance, his wings folding tightly against his back.

He screeches again, but his voice is now tinged with desperation. The display of brute force transitions into a calculated attack as he charges once more, but I am ready with countermeasures in mind.

As he approaches, I leap and dodge, claws poised and ready. But my mind finds only one thought—Arwen—and how every fight is meaningless without her. I have never been beaten, but tonight, the grip of my heart is far stronger than the grip of my claws. I need to get to her, but the only ticket out of this arena is through the death of your opponent and that won't fucking be me. I just found my Starlight and I'll be damned if I leave her on this earth unprotected. I'm her mate, her protector, her everything, so I need to kill this bastard by any means necessary to get my girl back.

With resolute determination, I summon every ounce of my energy and leap again, twisting just in time to evade Jasper's massive talon as it slashes through the air to meet me. I land solidly on the ground, my senses heightened, adrenaline coursing like fire through my veins.

The crowd is a swirling mass of agony and ecstasy. They want blood. They want chaos. With a sudden rush, Jasper lunges, and I can feel the wind from his wingbeats hitting me like a wall as I pivot just in time. His talons graze my shoulder, tearing through skin, but I growl with exhilaration instead of pain. Each bruise, each cut only fuels my resolve.

He thrusts his wings again, trying to slam me down, but I'm quick, dodging low before springing back up, ready to meet him. I charge forward, diving into the belly of the beast. Our bodies collide, and I land a pummeling blow against his abdomen, feeling his muscles tense beneath my strikes. The impact shocks us both mid-tangle, but the exhilaration of the fight sends my spirit soaring.

With unfathomable grit, I twist and throw a flurry of feral blows, each one fueled by the vision of her face streaked with tears but illuminated by courage. He recovers, infuriated, and I brace myself for the tempest. This time when he lunges, I don't dodge. Instead, I dig deep, my heart thrumming in sync with the battle, anticipating his every move.

We clash again, the sound of flesh tearing reverberating through the air, but I find myself overwhelming him, pushing him off balance and into the arena wall. I channel the rage and love that fuels my every strike.

As he falters, I see my chance. I pivot, redirecting my energy into one final assault, ripping through the air toward him. My claws find their mark, and the arena is steeped in silence as he crashes to the ground, his body lifeless beneath me.

The announcer's voice is a distant murmur, but victory fills my senses like a potent whiskey, sweet and numbing. It wraps around me, but shadowed emotions grip my heart. It's obscured by another outburst—a wave of terror washes over me, an insidious whisper in my mind that tugs at my very soul. I can feel her pain radiating through me. She's in danger. If someone dares to lay a finger on my precious mate, they will regret the day they were born.

I'm out of the ring, bounding toward the exit, my heart pounding erratically, overshadowing the cheers for my victory. The announcer's voice bellows through the speakers, but I don't care about the fucking money. The only true possession I have is Arwen, and I can't lose her.

I burst through the heavy wooden doors, a rush of adrenaline surging through my legs as I claw my way toward freedom. I shift quickly, grabbing a spare pair of clothes I find—rough-spun fabric that smells of sweat and leather—and barrel up the stairs, my arms moving with a life of their own.

"Fuck!" I growl. She's got her claws so deep in me. *What is it that makes me want to tie myself in knots to keep her safe?* All I can think about is that she's mine, and she needs a good hard fuck to teach her to behave.

My senses heighten, the sounds of the bustling bar fading into the background. I look in all directions for any signs of her. Her sweet scent of an ocean breeze is faint, but I know she was just here. It lingers in the air around me, a ghostly memory that makes my insides twist painfully.

I sprint through the dark alleys and crowded squares, fighting against the dwindling scent that beckons me. My eyes are scanning every corner, searching for any sign of her. I can feel the dark void expanding within me, a sensation that something—someone—is stealing my light.

Then, a muffled scream slices through the air, raw with terror, coming from a shadowy alley just ahead. Without a thought, I race forward, heart pounding, as dread coils tightly around my chest. I turn the corner to find a figure standing over Arwen, her arms tied tightly behind her with something shoved into her mouth. She's on her knees, looking up at the masked predator. Pain strikes through me as I lay eyes on her. Bruises mar her porcelain skin, desperation and defiance glittering in her eyes like shards of glass. Her glorious spirit who, even now, fights so fiercely against the shackles of despair. Fury ignites within me, roaring like a wildfire.

The assailant, a hulking brute dressed in dark leather, looms over her. "You think you can resist, little siren?" he hisses, voice dripping with contempt. My teeth grind, fury igniting like a wildfire within me.

"Get away from my wife!" I thunder, my voice a booming thunderclap, the earth seeming to quake beneath the force of my declaration.

The creature turns, surprised by my sudden appearance. His mocking grin fades to an expression of fury as he sizes me up. He draws a knife, glinting as he flicks it open, the blade flashing like a serpent ready to strike.

"This siren is mine. I've been searching for years. Her voice is the key to my domination," he seethes, placing the blade dangerously close to her throat.

Every instinct screams for me to protect her. In two swift strides, I close the distance, my fist connecting with his face—a satisfying crunch reverberates through my knuckles. He staggers back, shock morphing into immediate hatred. I follow up with a flurry of brutal strikes, each connection fueled by the rage and desperation to defend what is mine.

"You think you can take her from me?" I roar, striking again, punctuating each blow with the power of my feelings.

He swings wildly in retaliation, but I duck, my body reacting with instinctual swiftness. Anger whirls in my chest as I retaliate, delivering a swift kick to his side that sends him sprawling. The alley echoes with the sounds of our struggle—the grunts, the thud of flesh on flesh. I bend, pulling his back to my chest, circling my arm around his throat and squeezing. He claws at my arms and thrashes beneath me but I remain firm, tightening my hold more. He slowly begins to lose his strength until he's lying limp in my arms. I drop the bastard to the ground and turn toward my mate.

"Arwen!" I rush to her side and kneel down at her level. I take in her bruised face, the tears glistening in her eyes, cradling her face with my hands. "I'm here, my Starlight. I've got you."

As I untie her, she leans closer, and for a moment, just a moment, the shadows retreat. Her fingers tremble as she touches my cheek, her voice breaking free from the gag.

"You came for me. You found me," she whimpers.

I release a shuddering breath, knowing I will guard her against the night, for in her vulnerability lies a strength that can transcend darkness. "Always, Arwen. I'll always find you."

"He wanted..." she trails off on a sob.

"I know, baby. He will get what's coming to him." I promise, pulling out my phone to make a call to Gus Scott at the SRA. I've known him since I came to this city. He's helped me clean up more messes than I care to admit, but tonight I need his expertise in taking this bastard away and finding the true nature of his pursuit of Arwen. I need to know if there are others involved because I will stop at nothing until my love is safe.

"Mr. Scott, this is Black, sir. We have a situation. There's a masked man here that was hell-bent on finding a siren for his personal gain. He's unconscious for now, but I need him questioned and then thrown away," I explain, anger once again rising to the surface at the thought of his hands on her. Within minutes, agents arrive at the scene, detaining the assailant and carrying him away.

I lift Arwen from the ground, pulling her close to my chest as I walk her toward my car. Her trembling has faded but she clings to me like I may vanish in an instant. The valet sees me and takes off into the parking lot to bring my car around.

"Um..." She bites her lip as her cheeks flame.

"Yes?" I run my fingers along her cheek, brushing the silver-spun hair from her violet eyes. She's absolutely mesmerizing.

"Back in the alley," she begins. "You called me your wife," she whispers as if she's scared to speak the words aloud. I know what I said and I meant them.

"I did. You will be my wife, Starlight, but in my mind, you already are," I admit. A tear streaks down her face before I catch it on my tongue.

"Is this you asking me?" she taunts with a smile.

"No, baby. This is me telling you it's a done deal. You and me…" I pause, trying to find the right words. "We were two lost souls who wandered way too long looking for our other piece. I found you and I'll never let you go. You became a part of me the moment I saw you. Your shattered songs filled the cracks in my heart without knowing it. I love you, my little Starlight. *Today. Tomorrow. Forever.*" I press my lips to hers, tasting the salt of her tears.

A radiant smile breaks through her pain as she melts into my embrace. In this moment, the echoes of the arena, the scorn of the fights, and all I've sacrificed blur into insignificance. The fierce love that envelops us feels like an impenetrable shield against the darkness of my past. I no longer want to be the "Notorious Black." I want to be everything to Arwen, the protector of her heart, the sanctuary where she finds peace and happiness. I'll be the harmony to Arwen's melody.

Chapter Nine

Arwen

My mind is whirling with everything that's happened in the last week. After that man was carted away, Wilder received a flood of information about him. Nox Tenebris, a notorious Shadow Demon, had been terrorizing the city for years. His lair was a dilapidated mansion in a shady part of town, a place where no one dared to venture. When the Shifters Relations Agency (SRA) searched his home, they uncovered a chilling sight: other rare magical creatures he had imprisoned, their powers siphoned for his dark purposes.

Among the prisoners was a delicate fae with wings that shimmered even in the dim light, a young vampire who hadn't yet tasted blood, and a shape-shifter who could barely hold their form. Each had a story, a life disrupted by Nox's cruelty. Wilder volunteered to head the rescue operation. I think almost losing me shifted something inside him.

"What are you thinking so hard about, Starlight?" he asks, pulling me back against his chest and nuzzling into my neck. His intoxicating woodsy and leather cologne assaults my senses in the best way as I breathe him in.

"Just thinking of Nox," I murmur, hating the way my voice trembles. He spins me around in his arms, cupping my cheeks in his large, calloused hands.

"Listen to me. He will never hurt you again. *No one* will ever hurt you again," he clarifies, swiping a small tear from my face. I nod, unable to trust my voice with the rising waves of anxiety. Wilder moves his hands to my waist, lifting me in one swift motion then sits on the couch with me on his lap. I'm still amazed at the muscles on this man and the fact he can throw my chunky body around like a rag doll. I secretly love it. Wilder lifts my chin, forcing me to see the determination etched into his face. A wave of anxiety rolls through me not knowing what he's thinking about. I can feel tension coursing through us but I don't know if it's my feelings or his.

"I've let you have a few days to calm down from the shitshow of the other night, but there are some things we need to discuss," he implores, his gaze steady on mine. My cheeks flame, and I know it gives away my guilt I've been holding since running from that arena.

"I—"

"No, let me start. I want to know why you disobeyed me and ran." His voice is low and dangerous but not tinted with anger, more annoyance. His focus remains on me, expecting an answer. Suddenly my throat feels dry and my first instinct tells me to run and hide. I guess Jarrod did more damage to my psyche than I thought.

I blow out a deep breath, then begin, "I was scared," I admit, trying to pull my eyes from his. The intensity is too much for me to handle.

"No, you don't get to look away," he says, pulling my chin back. "Why were you scared?"

"I was so overwhelmed and never in a million years would I have expected that you would take me to an underground fight club. I hate violence," I say a little too loudly as my hands begin to tremble. Flashbacks of my whole life come crashing into my mind one by one. "That's all I've ever known and then seeing you in that ring, the raw savage energy surrounding you freaked me out. I can't do it. I don't want to see you like that. It all hit so close to home, I felt like I was suffocating and my mind told me to run, so I did." Everything spilled out so quickly that I have to suck in a deep breath of air. Wilder continues looking at me with a hard expression and it makes me feel small and vulnerable. *Maybe I'm too damaged for him? Maybe I'm not worth the hassle with all the extra mental baggage that comes with me.*

He sighs, running his hand down his face. "First, I want to tell you I'm sorry. I never would have taken you had I known it would be triggering," he admits with a solemn face. "Secondly, I gave you strict orders to stay with Kody. He was meant to protect you while I couldn't. When I looked up and saw you dashing through the crowd, a terror I've never felt before paralyzed me. I can't lose you, Arwen. I won't." Wilder closes his eyes for a moment, leaning his head back on the sofa. Time seems to tick away slowly as I wait for him to continue. A lump forms in my throat because I know I scared him but at the same time, I was terrified. It was a lose-lose situation.

"I know I messed up. If you want me to go—" His head snaps up, as heat radiates off of him in waves like the sun breaking through the clouds.

"Don't you dare finish that sentence, little girl," he warns, his tone sending chills of anticipation over my skin. His eyes darken, igniting with a fire that stirs something deep within me. He leans forward, his hands sliding up my arms, leaving trails of warmth in their wake.

"I think it's time you learn what happens when you don't do as you're told," he whispers into the shell of my ear.

"I'm your protector, your guide, your anchor. I know you've never had a role model, and that makes it even more important for you to trust in my strength and love. When you disobey me, it can put you in danger— something I cannot allow. I promised you this was forever, didn't I?" His words envelop me like a comforting blanket, so I nod.

"Words, Arwen," he commands, carrying an edge that urges me to comply, to submit.

"Yes." I swallow hard.

"Yes, what?" I hesitate, not knowing what he wants from me. The words hang in the air, taut with expectancy.

"Yes, sir?" I venture, as a thrill runs through me.

"Close. From now on I'm going to be your *Daddy*." His admission sends a jolt of electricity shooting through me. Tears pool in my eyes as I look up at my handsome mate, searching for any signs of insincerity, but all I find is determination and a hint of mischief. I bite my lip, trying to steady my voice.

"Really?" I ask, barely above a whisper. I've only read about this in books but it has always intrigued me. It feels surreal, the notion of surrendering so completely to him, yet an undeniable allure beckons me, whispering sweet promises of freedom from control.

"Yes, Starlight. I will be everything you've ever needed and more than you could ever fathom," he assures, running the back of his hand along my cheek. "Now, since we have that squared away, there's the little matter of your disobedience that has to be addressed." Wilder's eyes twinkle with mischief, igniting a wildfire of desire within me that grows hotter and more intense.

"Oh?" He laughs softly, a low, rumbling sound that sets my nerves alight with anticipation as he stands, effortlessly lifting me into his arms and carrying me toward the kitchen table

"Bend over, Starlight," he whispers, his warm breath ghosting over my neck like a whisper of promises yet to be fulfilled. Without a trace of hesitation, I lean over the formal dining table, as I rest my head, arms folded. The way he commands me makes my heart race, hunger pooling in my stomach.

In one swift motion, he rips my flimsy sleep shorts and underwear from my body, casting them to the floor.

"Mmm, look at that ripe cunt. It's always dripping for me, isn't it?" he growls appreciatively, igniting a blush across my cheeks as I clench my thighs together, desperately seeking friction to quell the ache within.

"Nu-uh, naughty girls don't get to come," he tsks playfully, a note of authority layered beneath the teasing. "Tell me what your safeword will be." All rational thoughts seem to flee my mind, scrambling for the answer he seeks, as heat emits through me.

"Umm … fire?" His chuckle rumbles from him, sending ripples of delight through my body. Fire was the only word that came to mind based on the molten lava that courses through me whenever he's near. Lately I'm always hot and needy for him, aching like I'll die if I don't get relief.

"Fire. Interesting choice. I know what my girl needs, but first…" He holds up rope in front of me, and I can feel the authenticity in his gaze. He is a master but also my protector.

"Put your hands behind you, little one." I turn back with confusion in my eyes. *Is he going to do what I think he is?*

Hesitantly, I draw my arms out from under my head, then push them behind me. Wilder's warm hands pull my wrists together and quickly ties them together. I wiggle my fingers, testing the bindings.

"You aren't getting out of that until I say so," he smirks, making me roll my eyes. "What was that, Starlight? Are you wanting more spankings than I originally planned?" I shake my head, causing a deep rumble of laughter to burst from his chest.

"I didn't think so. Now, count," he commands.

Without warning, the sting of his palm connects with my skin, echoing through the room like thunder. My ass is stinging from the spanking and I gasp, forcing myself up on my tiptoes.

"One," I squeak out, my body arching instinctively at his touch.

"Good girl," he praises, his voice smooth like rich velvet, melting my resolve further. Before I could collect myself, another slap rains down, and a moan escapes my lips. There's pain but also an underlying pleasure that has me backing up closer to him.

"Number? If you can't keep up then we will start over," he teases, the challenge present in his tone.

"Two!" I exclaim, the line between pleasure and pain blurring with each strike. He's got me twisted up so tight, I think I could come from just his touch. He caresses my throbbing skin, soothing the ache with his hands.

"Three more," he commands and with every strike, pleasure surges through me, making me teeter on the edge of bliss.

"Five!" I shout finally, a whimper escaping as I fight fiercely against the tidal wave of an orgasm crashing on me.

"You did so well. That wasn't so bad, was it?" he murmurs, his hands easing over my sore flesh, igniting patches of sensation across my body.

"No, *Daddy*," I tease, tasting the new name on my tongue, relishing in the way it hangs in the air between us. He growls in response, a primal, raw hunger that sends shivers dancing along my spine.

"You think you can just say that and not force me to ram my fat cock inside this tight little pussy?" My instinctual response is a choked whimper, the mere idea lighting a firestorm of need within me. As I hear his belt hit the floor, I look over my shoulder, seeing his barely restrained beast trying to surface. Our eyes lock, and a sadistic grin spreads across his face—one of the most intoxicating sights I have ever seen.

He moves closer, dragging his fingers through my wetness. *Who knew spankings would be such a turn on?* It makes me want to test his patience more often. A laugh bubbles up, but the next minute he's leaning over me.

"Don't you even think about it," he admonishes, leaning over me. "All your punishments won't be that easy." A thrill shoots through me and I know he can feel it too.

"What am I going to do with you?" he muses, his voice dripping with playful menace.

"Maybe stop reading my mind!" He laughs into my neck.

"But where's the fun in that?" he counters. Suddenly, he's positioned behind me, and with a powerful thrust, he plunges inside, filling me to the brim. The sound of the table screeching against the hardwood echoes around the room but it only fuels him further. He is like a man possessed, and I love every second of his forcefulness. He grips my hips possessively, thrusting with such force that the world around us seems to blur, reduced to mere rhythm and heat. I wish I had something to hang onto instead of my hands being tied behind my back, but something about being at his mercy has me ready to explode.

"Fuck, you squeeze me so well, Starlight," he grits out, his voice thick with dark pleasure. His desire twists around me like a serpent, enchanting and dangerous. He coils one arm around my waist and his fingers find my clit, expertly sending shocks of pleasure ricocheting through my body like pulse-beats of a mythical instrument. The sensations rise higher as his drive grows stronger. Pulsating heat engulfs me, and I feel myself spiraling down a plush rabbit hole of ecstasy, exploding into a magnificent sea of bliss that wipes away all thought. It is a world beyond reality—pure, throbbing ecstasy.

"That's my good girl, coming on Daddy's cock like the little slut you are," he encourages, his voice becoming more gruff and intoxicating, pushing me further over the precipice.

The boundaries of our worlds begin to blend, the ancient magic around us wrapping tightly into the fabric of our heated play. I can feel the enchantment swirling, the kind of magic that thrives on desires and sealed bonds. The world around us becomes a vivid tapestry of pleasure and pain, each thread interwoven with screams of bliss and whispered confessions.

He thrusts harder, deeper, claiming each part of me. My breath hitches, with each plunge awakening more desires within me, wrapping around us like a silken spell.

"Tell me how much you want my cum in this pussy," he growls, his voice drenched in lust, grounding perfectly against the backdrop of swirling fantasies in my mind. The intimacy of his words against the wild affection of our movements sends me spiraling into a blissful haze. My senses scream, and the urge to surrender becomes a physical roar within me.

"More than anything, Wilder!" I plead, drunk on the feelings only he can invoke.

"Damn right. That's the only place it belongs until you're carrying my child," he grunts as his force becomes erratic. He leans back, trailing his hand over my ass to the spot where no one has ever been.

"Soon, Starlight," he promises, pressing a finger

into my tight hole. The feeling is entirely foreign but not an unpleasant one. I gasp as a spark ignites somewhere inside, a feeling like a hot poker on my spine. He teases me mercilessly, probing deeper. Pleasure overshadows the initial discomfort, the stimulation is absolutely unworldly, pushing me even further over the edge, ready to erupt again.

He leans over, pressing me hard into the table, his need consuming him, his animalistic drive thrusting him deep inside my womb.

"It's too much. I can't come again," I whine.

"Yes, you fucking can. Squeeze your kitty around Daddy's cock and I'll give it to you. Come for Daddy," he urges as I feel him grow larger. His scent overpowers my senses, filling every space within me, surrounding my heart and soul. A feral roar releases as he pours inside me, and my own climax barrels into me.

I cry out as a sonic wave releases with my orgasm, the walls vibrating and quaking from my siren's song. I can barely hold on as the sensation rockets me further over the edge. Wilder's cock grows, the thick veins expanding. His cum becomes a lava flow, scorching my womb.

"Wilder!" I scream. He releases another harsh growl that vibrates down his cock and through me, continuing to release. We are locked together in a binding rhapsody, a melody no musician could hope to play. He pulses several more times, his slow movements turning rhythmic, becoming something trancelike.

"What have you done to me, Starlight?" He sighs as he carefully withdraws and I immediately miss his warmth. I am wrung out, sated, and utterly exhausted. Our combined juices begin to slide down my thigh but Wilder's hand is there pressing his cum back inside me.

He leans over me, untying the rope then kissing a

path along both wrists. His tongue swirls around each one, making me hungry for him all over again. He lifts me effortlessly, pulling me tightly to his chest, pressing his mouth to mine and kisses me slowly, thoroughly. Our bodies melt together with the movement, our union creating magic. He begins to walk us through the living room then up the stairs to the bedroom.

"What do you mean?"

He pulls back and his golden eyes bore into mine, an emotional torrent storms in his gaze.

"I never thought I could love again," he admits, a small smile playing on his lips.

"It seems impossible. A puma and a half-siren, half-human becoming fated mates," I muse.

He chuckles, and it sounds lighter and brighter.

"Because it should be, but you were made for me, the stars, gods and fates intervened for us." I sigh contentedly into his chest. He strokes a hand through my hair, and his essence wraps around me, protecting and soothing. He presses a kiss to my forehead before placing me on the bed gently.

"Sleep, little Starlight, dream only of our happily ever after."

My breath catches in my chest at his confession. The possibilities suddenly become clear. Fates, stars, destiny, I hadn't believed it existed but, *what if it is true?* This, what we share, is more than some random event, the chemical attraction of two compatible souls. It is an inconceivable yet inexplicable phenomenon, a force of cosmic magic I want to hold tight, forever.

Epilogue

Wilder

Six Months Later

Arwen's glow radiates around her, an ethereal light that seems to pulse gently in the ambiance of the restaurant. She draws my attention like the siren she is. The air shifts—a tangible enchantment igniting an undeniable stillness, holding the patrons in a collective breath, and under her spell, the bustling murmur of dinner conversation diminishes to a whisper.

Her long silken dress ripples with every graceful move, an extension of her beauty, while her silvery hair cascades down her back like a celestial waterfall, glimmering beneath the twinkling lights overhead. When I lean down to whisper in her ear, the warmth of her aura surrounds me, enveloping me in a sweetness that feels both intoxicating and safe.

"My little Starlight has everyone staring," I tease, watching the spark of annoyance flicker in her violet eyes. She lets out an aggravated huff, her delicate features twisting into a frown that only makes her more charming.

"They're staring because a fat whale just waltzed in here and interrupted their dinner," she argues, folding her arms defiantly against the delicate fabric of her bodice. Anger swirls through me like a tempest, the realization hitting me that she can't see her otherworldly beauty, the exquisite grace that reshuffles the world around her. Her swollen belly, a blissful testament of our love, intertwines the feelings further, heightening my attraction in ways I have yet to understand.

"Don't talk about my mate like that," I warn,

lifting my eyebrow, letting her know there will be repercussions if she continues down this path.

Her eyes narrow, but there's a flicker of something softer beneath the surface. "And what if I do?" she challenges, her voice licking with defiance yet laced with a sweet vulnerability that drives me wild.

I step closer, my hand gently cupping her cheek. "Then I'll have to remind you just how breathtaking you are," I murmur, my thumb brushing against her satin-soft skin, feeling the pulse of her warmth align with mine. "Every curve, every inch of you is perfect to me. And if you keep being a brat then Daddy will have to put you in place." I let the words linger, giving them weight deliciously heavy with promise.

Her cheeks flush, a delightful shade of pink blooming across her face, and for a brief moment, the crowd fades entirely, leaving us in this bubble of confession and playful tension.

"Maybe I like the attention," she says playfully, sticking her tongue out at me, her posture relaxing even as her defiant spark flares again.

I chuckle at her audacity, it ignites an entirely different kind of flame within me. "Just remember who you belong to, my Starlight. This glow? It belongs to me as much as it does to you. Let them admire, but I'm the one who gets to worship you in the night," I whisper, pulling her against me, wanting her to feel every inch of my desire. This is a bond only the two of us can share.

Her eyes soften, the tension in her shoulders easing as she leans into my touch. "You always know what to say," she whispers, a small smile tugging at her lips.

"That's because I mean every word," I reply, pressing a tender kiss to her forehead. "Now, let's enjoy this evening together, and let them stare. They can only dream of having what we have."

After our romantic dinner, I lead her from the restaurant, past the car and into a forest. She looks up at me with questions swirling through her beautiful eyes.

"I have a surprise for you and no, I won't tell you what it is." Her expression shifts to playful irritation, and her pout makes me laugh. I love when she gets feisty, but I stand firm, wanting her to relish this adventure I have carefully orchestrated.

The evening sun dips below the horizon, casting a golden glow that dances through the enchanted forest. The path ahead is lit by the soft luminescence of will-o'-the-wisps, guiding our way to a secluded clearing.

Hand in hand, we walk through the forest until we reach the center of the clearing, where an ancient stone circle stands, bathed in the ethereal light of the rising moon. In the center, a crystal-clear pool shimmers with magic, reflecting the starlit sky above.

She looks around, her eyes wide with wonder. "What is this place?" she asks, her voice filled with awe.

I chuckle softly, feeling a rush of warmth fill my chest. "This is a sacred place where wishes are granted and destinies are sealed," I answer.

Reaching into my pocket, I retrieve the small velvet box. The moonlight catches its edges, adding an aura of mystery. Taking a deep, steadying breath, I kneel by the enchanted pool, its soft glow reflecting in her eager, questioning gaze. She gasps, her hand flying to her mouth as tears shimmer in her eyes.

"Wilder..." she begins, disbelief threading through her tone, but I don't let her finish. Instead, I pour my heart out, the practiced words evaporating as raw emotion takes over.

"Starlight," I begin. "You are my world, my everything. You came into my life and imprinted yourself on my soul permanently just like the ink on my skin. Your essence filled my heart with an unbreakable bond. In a world filled with shattered melodies, you are the harmony that brings everything together. I am yours now and forever. Marry me."

The box slides open to reveal the breathtaking ring within. The band is crafted from shimmering platinum, intricately engraved with wave-like patterns that symbolize her siren heritage. At its center lies a stunning aquamarine gemstone, its serene blue hues reminiscent of the sea from where she came. Tiny black diamonds surround the aquamarine, representing my fierce black puma form, adding a touch of mystery and elegance to the design.

Her eyes widen even further as the words settle between us. "This ring embodies both of our worlds— your enchanting connection to the sea and my fierce love for you. Our passions are like ink on the pages of our hearts, indelible and profound. You turn chaos into a symphony, and I want to be with you for every note of it."

Her voice is a soft whisper, "Yes."

"Well, that's good because we're getting married now." Sliding the ring onto her finger feels like sealing a promise, an unbreakable vow made under the glowing gaze of the moon.

"What if I had said no?" she teases, brows raised playfully as I rise to stand before her, towering over her with my affectionate grin.

"That wasn't an option, Starlight. You're mine. And I'll spend the rest of my life proving it to you," I say earnestly, holding her gaze. The intensity of our bond echoes in the depths of her eyes, and as she looks down at the ring—the shimmering symbol of our shared journey—a spark ignites in the air around us.

"Now," I say softly, pulling her close, "let's make this night one to remember."

The forest stirs with life, as if alive to bless our union. The will-o'-the-wisps float closer, their soft glow casting an ethereal radiance over the clearing. I let out a short, melodious whistle into the night, my signal for our witnesses to emerge. From the shadows, Kit and Kody step forward, both of them exuding warm encouragement.

Kit, once Arwen's boss at the bar and now her closest friend, steps forward with a warm smile. The witch's aura shimmers with an iridescent glow, her eyes twinkling with joy. "I always knew you two were meant to be," Kit says, her voice filled with warmth. "Seeing you here, so happy and in love, is everything I hoped for."

Kody, my best friend, follows with a mischievous grin. "Well, well, Wilder. I never thought I'd see the day you found someone who could put up with you!" he teases, his eyes twinkling with humor. "But seriously, may your bond be as unbreakable as dragon scales, and may your love burn as brightly as my fire. You two are perfect together."

She turns back to me, joy dancing in her eyes, gleaming with disbelief yet filled with love. "I can't believe you put all this together," she whispers, her voice thick with emotion.

I grin wide, pulling her even closer, reveling in the moment we have created—the magic that radiates between us. "For you, I would do anything," I vow softly. "This is just the beginning of our forever."

****

In the quiet folds of the universe, where the celestial winds whisper secrets and the cosmos dance with a flicker of life, there exists a bond tethered by destiny itself. Her name was Arwen—a name that echoed in the chambers of my heart even before our paths intertwined.

From the moment I laid eyes on her, I recognized the fire within her spirit. She was defiant, thrumming with a wild energy, contrasting the gentleness of her features. Yet behind those bright, defiant eyes, lay fragments of a soul broken by carelessness and sorrow. She wore her pain like a second skin, and though her light shone fiercely, shadows lingered just beyond.

As I approached her, my heart beat in a rhythm that felt as if it had been sculpted from the very stars themselves, each pulse an echo of an ancient promise, the kind that writes itself into the firmament of the heavens. I knew at that moment she belonged to me. It was raw, a yearning so fierce it splintered the very fabric of reality.

I'd finally found my sweet little Starlight.

The End

CLAIM MY SOUL

Monsters of New York

Laura M. Baird

Copyright © 2025

Chapter One

Herleif Aganarsson began his night the same way he had for many nights the past year: annihilating monsters in the name of entertainment. Amusement for the rich, the elite shifters of New York, and the humans who were privy to the paranormal. Not that he gave a shit about entertaining the bastards, but he had no choice.

That's what happened when there was a debt to be paid. And a hefty one at that, thanks to his father's greed and ineptitude when it came to finances.

Herleif had struck a deal to pay that debt due to his aging father's decline in health as well as mental state. Thus, he began competing in the shifter fight club in the lower level of The Gin Room in New York City. Or rather, a suburb. Same difference in his mind. It was one of a handful of locations throughout the city.

To ensure his father, Agnar, made no more foolish decisions nor faced further temptations, he'd been forced to return to their homeland of Northern Denmark after making a rather large payment toward what he owed. Of course, he'd grumbled and protested, but at least Agnar still breathed.

There were times when Herleif himself had wanted to strangle his father for his fucking arrogance and brashness. But he was a devoted son and did what needed doing. His father seemed to take that for granted, but his mother had begged him for leniency and continued to express her gratitude. That eased his surly attitude for the most part. After all, there was little one could do when it came to failing mental capacities.

Then there were times his anger bubbled to the surface. That's when he'd channel that emotion and take his frustrations out on his opponents. And he never lost. That didn't stop other beasts or shifters from trying, thinking they'd best him. A few had come close, but at the end of the bout, he was always victorious, becoming a sure bet. Over the years, many had complained, and some had tried to prevent him from competing, but it'd been in vain.

Nothing and no one stopped Herleif the troll. Besides, he provided worthy performances for the viewers willing to toss an insane amount of money around.

If he had chosen to fight more often, he could've been done in less time. Good thing he hadn't been forced to pay the debt quicker, because even a battle-hungry troll couldn't stomach it every night. It lost its appeal. So, when he felt like it, he'd enter the club and go to work. Lately he'd been fighting more just to get the damn debt over and done with. He grew weary of this life and was ready to move on, doing what he wanted. What that was, he had yet to discover.

Per the rules of the club, he'd been rewarded handsomely, hence his decision to choose this activity to pay off the debt. Of course, he'd been allowed to keep a portion of the winnings in order to survive day-to-day. He hadn't needed much, living a minimalistic lifestyle by renting a hole-in-the-wall apartment located in the basement of a shifter-owned restaurant. A perk was all the leftover food that hadn't sold for the day, which was always plenty to fill his belly for the night.

"Harry! You're up!"

Herleif rolled his eyes at the shortened name, knowing nothing he said or did would change the action. In the beginning, he'd tried but soon realized it was a waste of his time and energy. Not that he had any shortage of energy. Trolls were notoriously known for their strength and stamina. He also had magical abilities, but it wasn't often Herleif needed to call upon that aspect of his being during a fight.

There were two arenas in this particular establishment where fights took place. The first being a roped section much like a boxing ring where competitors fought until one conceded. Then there was the pit which was exactly as one would think: a shallow hole in the rocky foundation where usually only one fighter exited alive.

Barbaric? Sure. But that was the way of it with many shifters. They needed an outlet, and this activity was regulated versus going out into the world and wreaking havoc among the humans. No one was forced to fight. It was always a choice.

Herleif was feeling especially surly tonight. He'd been on edge lately, angrier than usual, and he was ready to beat the shit out of someone. It was his nature, after all, and aggression was expected of him and his kind. But his father was setting him off. He'd been contacting Herleif more frequently, demanding he clear the debt and pave the way for him to return to the States. Agnar had become bored and restless, and he was ready for excitement.

Herleif's mother had no sway, and he felt sorry for her, living in committed misery to his bastard of a father. He'd tried ignoring Agnar but knew at some point he'd have to deal with him one way or another.

Lumbering his way to the pit, spectators—men and women alike—gave Herleif a wide berth while cheering as the announcer introduced him and his opponent. He paid them no heed as he focused on the man already standing in the shallow hole. He looked like an ordinary human, but Herleif knew looks were absolutely deceiving. He, for instance, had the ability to shift into human form, looking like a Viking of olden days, standing at nearly seven feet with dark blond hair and honed muscles from years of rigorous training and fighting. In his true form as a troll, he could double as the widely popular Green Giant from the comics. That is, if said giant had long hair, clawed hands, and tusks protruding from his mouth.

Leaping into the pit, the ground shook beneath Herleif's feet, causing his opponent to stumble. But the man immediately shifted into a wolf, snarling and hissing as the crowd gathered closer, shouting with enthusiasm.

"Lycan, eh? Time to teach a dog to heel." Herleif baited, knowing it'd irk the beast. He'd fought numerous shifters, from vampires to wraiths to a variety of animals, so he was no stranger to wolves. This one was the largest to date but still small compared to Herleif. Usually he fought with no weapons, using only his brute strength, and most bouts didn't last long. On occasion, spears, clubs, and shields were thrown into the arena, and the fighters—even Herleif at times—took full advantage of their use.

The wolf prowled, jaw snapping and fur bristling as Herleif circled, watching and waiting for him to make the first move. After several moments, the crowd grew restless, taunting and growling almost as much as the Lycan, encouraging action. The beast shifted left then right, lunging at Herleif's ankles, only to receive a kick for his efforts. Credit to the wolf, he didn't whine but took the blow, rolling and springing up onto his paws. He snarled, lunged again, only to flip in midair, kicking out with his hind legs, catching Herleif on the arm. Scratches welled with blood and the crowd roared with excitement.

Herleif merely glanced at his arm then grinned at the Lycan. "First strike. It'll be your last." He feigned a lunge causing the wolf to jump back. That's when Herleif made his move, punching the beast in his jaw. This time, the wolf couldn't contain his cry, but he managed to scurry away before Herleif could land another blow.

The two circled one another, getting in strike after strike and each taking a few tumbles. Then with speed that impressed Herleif, his opponent jumped on his back and tried to latch onto his shoulder. But Herleif grabbed the Lycan and tossed him over his head so that he landed with a sickening thud against the rocky floor. Herleif inwardly winced at the impact but couldn't show weakness. Instead, he merely smirked.

And why did that still leave a sour taste in his mouth?

The beast remained unmoving as Herleif approached with caution, knowing he could be faking unconsciousness to draw him closer before striking.

Labored breaths escaped the wolf's mouth along with a gurgling that probably meant internal bleeding. Herleif felt sorry for the creature. Suddenly, he transformed back into a man and began to spit up blood. When his gaze met Herleif's, he could barely keep his eyes open.

"Mercy. Don't let him take my soul," he croaked

before a wracking cough overtook him, causing more blood to spew onto the ground.

Herleif stiffened at that remark. Who would take his soul? Wouldn't it ascend like all the others?

"Finish me," the Lycan rasped.

Herleif looked around at the cheering crowd as they yelled for the man's death. In that instance, he wanted to decimate the spectators, wipe them out for finding pleasure in his acts.

Seeing nothing or no one unusual, he kneeled, about to do something he'd never done before. Clasping his hands on either side of the warrior's head, Herleif met his gaze. "Till Valhalla," he whispered. Then snapped the man's neck, giving him a quick death.

Herleif hung his head, letting his hands drop as he took a deep breath. For a brief moment, he tuned out the roar of the crowd and their gleeful delight over another kill, sending up a prayer for the shifter. He wasn't especially proud that he'd ended the lives of many over the years, and now he grew weary of it all, eager to leave this servitude in two months. Or less.

Gaining his feet, he threw his head back, releasing a bellow that rocked the room. The crowd roared, obviously thrilled with the battle, mistaking Herleif's grief for pride in his triumph. When he lowered his head, he met the gaze of emerald eyes filled with sorrow. A woman stood among the crowd in partial shadows, but her form was impossible to miss.

He'd never seen her before and briefly wondered who she was. Suddenly her eyes flared with a golden light, startling him with its intensity. But when another light caught Herleif's attention, he knew what he would see, as he'd seen it every time he ended a life. Looking down upon the man, a luminescent mist began rising from the body. It contained pinpoints of light, like a swarm of fireflies, and when he followed its path, it began to weave through the crowd. Herleif never knew if others ever saw it, or if they didn't care, because their focus always turned to the next shifters approaching the pit.

With a burst of speed *he'd* never seen before, the light shot straight for the woman. Herleif jerked, ready to shout a warning, but she simply absorbed the light, appearing unaffected. Then she blinked and tears from her green eyes tracked down her rounded cheeks.

What the hell?

Herleif made a move in her direction, but the sea of bodies swallowed her like a ship lost to a storm.

VOLUME THREE

Chapter Two

Alexia Stavros pulled the hood of her coat over her head, fading into the background. She carefully yet quickly worked her way toward the stairs and when clear of everyone, used her magic to veil herself.

Tonight had been her first time in the fight club, and after being briefed, she thought she'd known what to expect. It certainly hadn't been to absorb the energy of the fallen shifter. Her purpose was to guide the souls to the afterlife, which she'd done countless times before. Well, before coming here. And she had been successful with the Lycan. But never before tonight had she felt a life force flow through her with such intensity before ascending.

Why had tonight been different?

And then to have the troll focus on her. Herleif. Had he been a factor?

There was no mistaking he had seen what arose from the Lycan. Had the others? It hadn't appeared so. Only Herleif had followed the spirit as it wound its way toward her while everyone else carried on as if nothing unusual were happening. For a fleeting moment, he had looked panicked, fearing something awful would happen to her. And when it was over, he had looked … astonished.

Alexia's thoughts were interrupted by a deep shout. Heavy footfalls rattled the steps she'd begun to climb. Although still invisible, she didn't dare look behind her. Instead, she rushed up the remaining stairs and darted into a secret room she'd been shown when given a tour of the club. Darkness swallowed her as she carefully listened for any indication Herleif was trailing her.

Muffled voices and rushed footsteps made their way to her, but she wasn't discovered while tucked away. Even after it grew quiet, she continued to wait while her thoughts pondered what she'd been told regarding The Gin Room.

Not all were in agreement that the fight club should operate as it did or even at all. But it had been this way for nearly a century and didn't seem likely to change. Fighters had the choice of surrender or death. Some chose a fight to the death. Whether it was due to their brazenness, thinking they couldn't lose, or possibly out of desperation, not wanting to continue in this life, she couldn't say nor judge. Either way, the reward was great. For those who perished, a portion was paid to a person of their choosing, typically a family member.

She wondered about Herleif and his reason for fighting. For enjoyment? A release of his aggression? And how often did he compete?

From his impressive strength to surprising agility, Alexia could admit he'd been magnificent. His movements were fluid despite his size, and to watch his muscles flex with his competent display … she felt herself blushing just thinking about the performance. His show of mercy had been commendable. His remorse tender. The crowd hadn't keyed in on that, but she certainly had.

Noise outside the door brought Alexia's attention back to her predicament. If Herleif had tried to locate her, she hoped she'd waited long enough that he'd given up or moved on. He didn't strike her as one to easily abandon a task, but she couldn't stay here all night.

Easing open the door, she listened for voices or movement. When nothing seemed amiss, she removed her cloak of magic and slid into the corridor. Remaining vigilant, she skirted the dance floor, winding her way around tables and toward the exit. A few steps from the door, her path was blocked, and when she looked up, it was her uncle, Nic Stavros. He placed a hand on her arm and gently guided her toward the back where a table awaited with food and drink. She'd forgotten he requested to meet with her after she was done below. Without needing to be told, she took a seat as he did the same.

"What happened?" he asked softly. "You weren't down there very long."

Her gaze flickered to the crowd before she met her uncle's gaze. "The shifter's soul was clearly seen leaving his body, but only by myself and the troll, Herleif. There was no reaction from anyone else, no indication they'd seen the beautiful light that shot straight through me. *I'd* never seen anything like it. I'd never *felt* anything like it."

"And now?"

She shook her head. "I don't feel any different now than any other time I've done this."

"Something else happened."

She gave a quick nod. "Herleif. He saw me. His gaze was intent as if he knew I had something to do with what happened. I think he tried to follow me. Did you see him come through here?"

Her uncle shook his head. "I did not. He may have gone out the back or simply given up."

Alexia scoffed. "He does not strike me as a being that would give up on anything." She took a drink of the water in front of her. "What do you know of him?"

"I know he's been fighting for a year, paying off a debt owed by his father."

"And the Lycan? His name is, or *was*, Evan Hosten. Why was his death any different?"

"I don't know anything about the wolf, but I'll

find out." He paused, contemplating. "Maybe it had nothing to do with the wolf but with Herleif himself. What was he doing when it happened?"

"I wondered that very thing because it was what he'd done *before* it happened that may have had an influence. He gave the werewolf a mercy killing. They were clearly fighting to the death, battling one another hard. When Herleif slammed the wolf to the ground, he'd done immense damage. Then the wolf shifted back to human form. Even amidst the noise of the crowd, I heard him say, *finish me*. Herleif framed his face and whispered, *Till Valhalla* before snapping his neck."

"Very admirable."

"Uncle Nic," she started again in a hushed voice, "something else was said by the wolf. Something disturbing. He said, *Mercy, don't let him take my soul*."

If her uncle was alarmed, he gave nothing away.

"You're sure?"

She nodded. "I am."

"Are you okay?"

"Just tired," she sighed.

He reached across the table to take her hand. "Let me get someone to escort you home. I'd do it myself, but I have another matter with work to finish up."

Her uncle worked for the Shifters Relations Agency in New York City, which regulated shifter activity. They also kept peace among their kind and the humans who'd become aware of the paranormal. Alexia had only been in the city a handful of months, having come over from Greece at the insistence of her parents who thought she needed to experience the modern world. She had stayed with her uncle and his family for two months, becoming familiar with the city and this new way of life. Now she had a place of her own in Hunters Point which was across the East River from his townhouse in Manhattan. Her apartment was close to the local library where she spent a great deal of her leisure time. Even though she'd been enjoying this world, there were many days and nights when she missed the slower pace of life on her island of Karpathos.

"Alexia, don't fret about tonight. While it isn't a normal occurrence, it doesn't mean there's anything ominous about the event. I'll do some checking, and we'll talk tomorrow. Now, let me find someone—"

"It's okay, Uncle Nic, I'm fine to get home. I could use a walk. While I haven't had any concerns thus far, I'll veil myself just in case." Her place was only a half mile from The Gin Room which was located in Gotham Point just past the Midtown Tunnel. When he gave her a concerned look, she tried again to ease any worry. "Really, I'll be all right, and I'll contact you as soon as I'm safely locked away for the night."

"Okay, but be sure to text me the moment you get to your apartment."

She nodded. "Promise."

Both stood and embraced before Alexia headed for the door. She was stopped by the bouncer, Dax, who was a panther shifter and apparently a big, friendly flirt according to most of the waitresses.

"Leaving so soon?" he said. "I haven't had a chance to buy you a drink yet."

Alexia gave a weak smile. "Maybe another night."

Dax gently grasped her hand and kissed it before releasing. "I'll hold you to that." He winked. "Are you fine to get home alone or is your uncle escorting you?"

She shook her head. "I'm fine, truly. Uncle Nic has work to do and I'll be veiled."

Dax nodded even though his look said he wasn't too happy about the decision. "Be vigilant. I'm sure you can handle yourself, but there's always strange activity during the full moon. And with Samhain upon us, it gets even stranger."

"Don't I know it." She chuckled. "But thank you for your concern. I'll be okay, and I promised Uncle Nic I'd text him as soon as I'm safely in my apartment."

He nodded. "Will I see you tomorrow night?"

"I'm not sure yet, but if so, I may take you up on that drink."

"You got it." He grinned, showing a perfect set of gleaming white teeth.

After a final good night, Alexia slipped out into the crisp yet humid October air. Ensuring no one was around to witness her magic, she cloaked herself and began to walk up 2nd Street. She'd take it until it ended then skirt the park before ending up at her apartment building.

She thought about the food she'd ignored. When her belly rumbled, she chuckled to herself, realizing she hadn't eaten all day and was suddenly famished.

With food on her mind, she'd walked a few blocks when she felt a presence. Freezing in place, an imposing figure stepped out of the shadows to loom in front of her.

"Care to explain what happened back there?"

Herleif.

Chapter Three

Herleif half expected the woman to startle or run or … something. But she held herself still, as if doing so would mean he wouldn't know where she stood. She may have the ability to make herself invisible to others, but for whatever reason, he could still see her. Mostly. Her form was like an apparition slightly out of focus.

It still didn't prevent him from seeing just how alluring she was. Standing barely a foot shorter than him, she was taller than most women he'd met. Her hood covered what he knew was dark auburn hair, but he could clearly see her round face, full lips, and those emerald eyes that held strength and determination. And they bored into him with a look of suspicion.

He stepped into the meager light from a streetlamp. "You may as well drop your magic. I can see through your cloak."

She took a step back. "If you can see me, why bother to show myself? Maybe I don't want anyone else to see me." She spoke low in a calm manner, her sultry voice causing his blood to heat. But was it in lust or irritation?

"You mean you don't want anyone to see you speaking with me. A troll."

He watched her cute little nose wrinkle. "You being a troll has absolutely nothing to do with it. Maybe you shouldn't be seen speaking with a witch."

"Is that what you are? A witch?"

She lifted her shoulder in a careless shrug. "Some would call me that."

He took a step closer, only to have her retreat that step. "And why should I not be seen speaking with you?"

She hesitated a moment before stepping further

away from the light, causing her appearance to fade slightly. Herleif wanted to protest, wanted to beg her to show herself, but she began to speak again. "Even in today's world of acceptance among the paranormal, witches are still given a wide berth, it seems. And I'm new here, most don't know me, so they could be wary of me."

"Have you given others a reason to be wary of you?"

"No," she said, quickly defending herself.

"Then show yourself. While I appreciate you worrying about my reputation, I don't give a fuck what anyone thinks." When she narrowed her eyes but remained silent, he gave a low growl while stepping closer. "I want answers, woman. What happened back in the pit?"

"I don't know," she ground out.

Herleif boxed her in, staring down at her, and still she didn't flinch. "You lie. You know exactly what happened."

"S-step away from me." Her voice was low, husky, and adamant, even with that little wobble.

"And if I don't?" He goaded.

Before he could take his next breath, she had raised her hands and propelled him backward by an unseen force. He heard her gasp as he landed on his ass across the street from where she stood. When he looked up at her, she had dropped her veil, and her eyes were wide with surprise. Then there was the fact that a blue light glowed from her hands.

"I-it's not my intent to harm you, but don't ever call me a liar or intimidate me again. Next time, I won't be so easy on you."

Herleif stood and began to march toward her. He could've sworn he heard a growl of warning as if coming from a dog or wolf, but he saw neither. When the blue light in her hands changed to fireballs, he stopped and met her gaze, which now showed conviction.

"Do not challenge me, Herleif."

"It seems unfair that you know my name, yet you failed to give me yours."

"I failed at nothing. I only know your name because it was announced in the club. Giving you my name would imply a rather cordial relationship, when in fact there's nothing cordial about this so far."

"I want answers." He growled again.

"So you said, and I have none for you. What happened earlier has never happened before. Maybe it's *you* who has some explaining to do." She continued to hold the fireballs in her palms while keeping a keen eye on him.

"Me? I had nothing to do with the light that came from the Lycan's body. While I've seen the life force leave the fallen, I've never seen it target an individual. And before tonight, I've never seen you in the club. So, tell me, who should be doing the explaining?"

"I owe you nothing, so it appears we're at a standstill and have no need for further conversation."

When she started to lower her hands, Herleif reacted, sprinting forward with a speed that surprised her. She grunted when he locked his hands around her wrists, pinning them above her head against the wall at her back. He crowded her body with his, so much that he felt every desirable inch of her curves.

"Release me," she ground out.

Herleif had to commend her for her spirit, but he had no intention of releasing her until he got answers. He lowered his head so his mouth was next to her ear. "I don't think I will." He barely got the last word out when he received a brutal kick in the crotch. Fumbling backward, he released her hands and was once again shoved away by her magic, landing in the street. A bright light shone on him, yet he had no time to react to the vehicle barreling down on him.

Suddenly, he found himself hovering in the air while the truck sped by as if the driver hadn't just seen a troll lying in its path. Seconds later, he was dropped across the street, and when he turned his head to look at the witch, she was nowhere to be seen.

****

Alexia leaned against the door inside her apartment, perplexed. Normally after teleporting, she would've been exhausted since it expended more energy than any other act she performed. It wasn't often she had need of that power, but she didn't want to hang around on the street and continue tangling with Herleif. Especially when he wouldn't heed her warning.

She wasn't lying when she said she didn't want to hurt him, but she almost had. The burst of power she'd unleashed not only shocked him, but herself as well. She was powerful in her own right, but where had that extra intensity come from?

The energy of the Lycan she'd felt herself absorb? Had it become a part of her?

How? Why?

Even after that first push, Herleif wouldn't back down. Despite her anger with him, she'd reacted quickly enough to save him from that delivery truck. Then again, given his size, he might have been fine. The truck, probably not. But the last thing she wanted tonight was an incident involving a human which would've meant her uncle or someone else from the SRA showing up.

Making her way to the couch, she pulled her

phone out of the pocket of her coat. She sent a text to her uncle, letting him know she was safely home and headed straight to bed. She absolutely would not worry him about her encounter with Herleif. She was fine, Herleif was fine, but neither were any closer to finding the answers they sought.

Uncle Nic replied, wishing her a good night and that he'd contact her tomorrow.

Alexia dropped the phone beside her and closed her eyes as she leaned back against the cushions. She'd see what information, if any, her uncle could provide regarding the Lycan and Herleif before she considered telling him about tonight. She wouldn't have minded a civil conversation with the troll. Too bad he wasn't having it.

Her thoughts turned to their interaction mere moments ago and how quickly it'd escalated from almost polite to downright rude. The nerve of him, trying to intimidate her. And not believing her words. It's not like she could pull answers out of her ass hoping he'd be satisfied with them. She'd told the truth. She couldn't help it if he didn't like it any more than she didn't like what he'd had to say.

Alexia felt herself smile as she again thought of Herleif's surprise at her power and that she'd dared to use it on him. But once her own shock had worn off, she'd been adamant about him backing away. She would not allow him to assert any kind of authority over her.

"Ha, take that, you big oaf," she mumbled. "Like women should just roll over and be complacent to men. I don't think so," she said through a yawn.

Before she grew too tired to move, she forced herself to get up. Removing her coat, she hung it on a peg then walked to the kitchen. Her stomach made it known it wasn't pleased to have been neglected, so she ate enough to satisfy it before heading to her room. She tried to put thoughts of Herleif and the evening out of her mind, knowing she wouldn't get any more answers right now.

"A good night's rest is what's needed, then I'll regroup tomorrow."

She didn't bother with her nighttime routine as she stripped off her clothes and crawled into bed. Burrowing under the covers, all thoughts of the evening vanished as sleep overtook her.

Chapter Four

"They need you, Alexia. You must save them."

One moment Alexia was sound asleep, and the next, she was surrounded by a faint light, listening to the echo of a voice in distress. She knew she wasn't here in physical form, more like her subconscious was here in a dreamlike state. But how? And where was *here*?

And who needed her?

"The souls need your guidance."

Humans thought in simplistic terms. Heaven or Hell. That is, if they believed in an afterlife for their soul. But it wasn't as simple as that. Oh, she wished it was, though. A soul's journey didn't end upon death. There were realms to negotiate based on an individual's behavior in life. Her purpose was to guide souls on their destined path in the afterlife. More often than not, she hoped it was to Heaven, but that was up to Fate to decide. When guiding, she could feel their essence and knew where they were headed. Like the Lycan last night. Although his spirit felt disturbed at first, she knew he had gone to Heaven.

And it wasn't often she'd been called upon to redirect a soul.

When first made aware of the powers she'd come into and her role in the cosmos, she had asked why it was even necessary.

"Souls are like wayward children," her mother had said. "When not anchored in a body, they know not of their purpose and therefore need instruction. It is as if their memories are wiped, not remembering their life in the physical world. It is your duty and others like you to move them in the direction Fate ordains."

"Was that your role also?" she'd asked her

mother.

"It was, but now it is time to pass that role onto you. Just as you will do with your daughter. Just as all the women in our line have done."

"But what if I don't have a daughter? What if I don't want a mate?"

Her mother had simply chuckled. "My dear, your fate is written, and our lineage will not end with you."

Alexia had contemplated that and so began the deep discussion about fate versus choice and what is preordained. At the time, it'd been overwhelming. It still was, to be honest, but Alexia had learned there is always a choice, and whether one chose to believe that was the choice that was destined … well, it made her head swim, so she didn't dwell on it. All she knew was to make the best choice when faced with options and let what will be, be.

Now, to determine what she faced and why.

"You must free the souls."

The disembodied voice came from all around her, and Alexia knew she wouldn't find its source. Just as she wasn't going to discover where she was. Didn't seem to matter at this point. There were other pressing details to learn.

"Where are these souls and why must I free them?"

"They are not where they belong. A soul collector is at work, upsetting the balance."

Soul collector? Alexia had never heard of such a thing.

"You are the guide. You have the power. But you will need help."

"Help? From whom? If I have the power, why would I need help?"

"You will need the allegiance and protection of

the one who sees the true you."

That sent a little jolt through Alexia. "Sees the true me?" she murmured. "I don't understand. Why do I need protection?"

"It is a perilous task, but he will not forsake you."

"He?" Alexia felt as if she'd leave here with more questions than answers. "Who are you? Why aren't *you* freeing the souls?"

"I am simply Fate's messenger. The power is not within me."

"Yet you had the power to summon me … here."

"I am a dream walker and do Fate's bidding."

"And Fate cannot intervene?"

"It has not come to that. Yet."

Alexia knew Fate to be an impartial being. Had to be. But would there ever come a time when she'd have to step in? Apparently, Alexia and her mysterious partner, protector, or whatever she was to call him, were the first in line to undo the work of this soul collector.

"How am I to know who this partner will be, and how do we find the soul collector?"

"The one who sees you when others cannot. There is more to the troll than even he realizes."

"Herleif? *He* is to be my protector?" Alexia wasn't so much alarmed as she was annoyed. She had to work with that stubborn scoundrel?

"He will not forsake you."

"Yes, you said that. I'm sure he'll be just as thrilled as I am to learn about this arrangement," she murmured. "Is there any more you can tell me? Where is this soul collector? How do we stop him?"

"Together, you'll know what to do."

"That's it?" Alexia was met with silence. Before she could ask another question, a burst of light flashed as a soft whooshing popped her ears. She jerked upright in her bed, once again surrounded by darkness. Her breaths were quick, and it took a moment for her eyes to adjust and realize where she was. She started to reach out with her senses, but movement in the shadows had her hands flaring with her fireballs. She then felt the presence and heard the growls of her spirit companion, Nonia, a wolf-dog, who materialized at her side.

Raising a hand, the room illuminated, revealing a hulking figure in front of her balcony doors. The man had dark blond hair with braids framing his temples, and his face was covered with a mustache and beard. He wore a tan shirt and dark pants that molded to impressive muscles, while black boots covered his feet. When Alexia looked into his striking blue eyes, a hint of recognition had her frowning.

"Herleif?"

Nonia barked, but it was one of excitement. Next thing Alexia knew, her wolf-dog leapt off the bed and raced to their uninvited visitor, or rather, intruder, in her eyes. Herleif knelt and greeted the beast no one else should have been able to see, much less touch. But he ran his hands over her head then back and forth across her sides, delighting Nonia.

Alexia softly harrumphed, only to hear the chuckle of the troll. Or man. And why was he in human form?

She used her magic to light several candles on her side tables before extinguishing her fireballs.

"Why are you here? And how did you get into my room?"

She heard the soft command of "Return" before he stood, his eyes locking on hers. Nonia returned to the bed, nestling against Alexia's side. Herleif's gaze roamed across her form, and she noticed his fists clenching at his sides. When his eyes met hers again, she felt her nipples tighten at the intensity, and only then did she remember she was naked.

She yanked the covers over her upper body and watched as Herleif flexed his hands again while keeping their gazes locked.

"Why are you here, Herleif, and why are you in human form?"

"I think you know why I'm here. Alexia."

She sucked in her breath as her pulse accelerated. "How did you learn my name?"

He took a step closer causing Nonia's tail-wagging to increase. "Stay," Alexia commanded.

"Did you dream tonight, Alexia?"

She pinched her lips, knowing what he hinted at but hated his roundabout way of answering her. "What does that have to do with why you are here?"

More steps brought him to the edge of her bed. "Do not play dumb with me, woman."

Now Nonia let out a soft whine, and Alexia sank her fingers into her fur, soothing her. "It's okay," she whispered to her companion before facing Herleif again. "Fine," she bit out. "No, I did not dream, but I was pulled into a dreamlike consciousness."

"And?" he prompted.

Alexia sighed. "*And*," she drew out, "it seems we are tasked to work together to save souls."

VOLUME THREE

Chapter Five

Herleif tried to calm himself.

He was unsuccessful.

Seeing Alexia's naked torso had him hard. Aching. Yearning.

He'd wanted to rip the covers from the bed in order to expose all of her glorious body. He'd wanted to drink in her beautiful sight before he claimed her, marked her, and made her his for all eternity.

Where the hell were these feelings coming from? He'd lusted after women simply for sex, but this intense, dare he say, *emotion*, was baffling. Disturbing.

Consuming.

"Herleif!"

The bark of his name pulled him out of his lust-induced haze to see her standing, fully clothed, two steps from him.

"Why are you in human form?" she asked again.

He smirked. "Is this not more appealing?" All other women he'd encountered preferred it.

She frowned. "No."

That one word gave him pause. Dare he believe she'd rather see him as a troll? He instantly shifted back to his true form, earning a happy yip from Nonia. He didn't know how he knew the wolf-dog's name, he just did. He'd learned Alexia's name from the dream walker who visited him earlier, no doubt the same one who had come to her.

Herleif studied her face as her gaze raked over him, all expression masked. That is, until her emerald eyes met his, and in them he saw a flare of longing. But in the next instant, she blinked and turned away, hiding from him.

"Alexia," he called, but received no response as she left the bedroom, Nonia at her heels. He followed her into the kitchen area where she'd turned on dim lighting.

"Would you care for anything? I'm having tea."

"Being cordial now, are ya?" he teased as he leaned against the archway.

Alexia whirled and glared at him "Do not start with me, Herleif. You were disrespectful earlier, and now you come into my home uninvited as if you have every right to do so. I should put you out on your ass again, you big jerk."

She'd marched right up into his personal space and poked him in the chest, not the least bit intimidated by him. He wanted to laugh at how cute he found it, instead he took hold of her hand, wrapped an arm around her waist, and hauled her against him. Her breath rushed out, and he felt its warmth on his chest. When she began to struggle, he groaned at the feel of her body wiggling against him. His cock ached and his grip tightened.

"Stop," he barked.

She fought even more, trying to free herself. "Don't yell at me!"

Nonia gave a low growl, but Herleif ignored her. "Then do as I say," he ground out.

"Like hell I will. Let me go."

He whispered in her ear, "And if I don't want to?" Her movements stilled, but he felt the shiver run through her body. "I happen to like you right where you're at. In my arms. Against my body." He dared to lick the shell of her ear and delighted in her soft moan. His hand caressed her low back, and she pressed her body closer.

"W-what are you doing to me?" she whispered as her free hand clutched his shirt.

He leaned back to look at her face and saw no fear, only curiosity. "Seducing you. Trying hard not to ravage you like the beast I am."

"You … you want me?" Her face held genuine surprise, perplexing Herleif.

"Is that a joke?" When Alexia shook her head, he asked, "Has no one ever desired you? Stated their interest in you?"

"No. I…" She lowered her head. "I was never around men until I came to New York."

Herleif gently touched her chin and raised her head so their eyes met. "How is that possible?"

"It just is. I remained close to my family, my parents, on our island."

Nonia had settled, seemingly satisfied her mistress was fine.

Herleif stroked her cheek, loving the silky feel of her skin. "Were you never curious about men? About sex?"

Alexia's cheeks blushed beautifully, and she tried to look away, but he held her chin and her gaze. "Alexia?"

"Of course, I was curious about s-sex. I guess I figured one day…"

"One day?" he prodded.

"That it'd happen," she blurted out, blushing a deeper red. "Silly, I know."

"Not silly," he said kindly, meaning it. "But in order for *it* to happen, there must be a male involved." He tried not to show his astonishment at realizing she was a virgin.

She narrowed her eyes. "I know that. I'm not clueless. It's not as if I haven't—" She suddenly clamped her mouth shut.

"Haven't what? Been educated? Read about it?" He lowered his voice. "Experimented by yourself?"

Her eyes widened as her mouth formed that

perfect O, and all Herleif could think about was filling that cavity with his cock.

"Herleif!" she snapped.

"By the gods, I love when you say my name. Whether in anger or in question." He brought his face to her neck, inhaling her sweet scent of arousal that stirred his blood and caused his cock to become hard as granite. "How I'd love to hear you scream my name in ecstasy." He licked her galloping pulse. "Would you like that, Alexia? Would you want your first time to be with me? A troll?"

She reared back, surprising him with the stern look on her face. "Why do you do that? Why must you be so self-loathing?" When he loosened his grip, she stepped back further, raking her gaze down his body then back up again. "Is there something wrong with you? Are you ashamed of who you are?"

He bristled. "Never."

"Then stop making it sound as if being a troll is abhorrent. Because it's not."

Rather than think too hard about her words and how they warmed the depths of his soul, he reverted to his usual snarky arrogance. "Does that mean you'd welcome me in your bed?"

"Ugh!" She threw her hands up in exasperation and returned to the task of getting mugs and tea out of her cupboards.

Herleif held back a laugh as he watched her backside, enjoying the view of her curves and her long hair swaying with her movements. His mind took an erotic turn and quickly had to shut down those thoughts. Otherwise, he would have her on her hands and knees as he plowed into her from behind.

And that wouldn't begin to slake his thirst for her. It certainly wouldn't be what she deserved, which was to be cared for, treated with tenderness. To be loved.

Herleif didn't know if he was capable of love. Lust, yes, most definitely. But love? That involved vulnerability. Trust.

"If you're a coffee drinker, then too bad. Tea will have to do."

Herleif's thoughts returned to Alexia's task. "Tea would be fine. Thank you."

She turned to face him, her brow raised as if she couldn't believe he'd been polite.

"What? I do have some manners." He grinned.

She scoffed, but he caught her grin as she turned to prepare the tea. Herleif moved closer and leaned against the counter, simply watching as she moved about, pulling food from the fridge while the water heated. Within moments, the drinks were ready, and she'd arranged meat, cheese, and fruit on a plate she set on the counter between them.

Her gaze met his and she smiled softly. "I figured food was also in order, given it's nearly dawn and time for breakfast. Are you hungry?"

"Famished," he said, and he wasn't talking about the need for food. But he reigned in his lust and thanked her for her efforts. "I rather like us being cordial to one another," he said, using her words, earning a grin.

"Well, Herleif Aganarsson, let's talk about our mission." She popped a grape in her mouth then smiled wider. "Am I correct that you were also visited by Fate's messenger and informed of what's expected of us?"

He nodded. "To save souls from a soul collector."

"I was told, together we'd know what to do. So, how do you propose we find this soul collector?"

Herleif frowned. "I have no idea. Why should I know what to do?"

"Because the dream walker said so."

"Oh, well, in that case, I guess I should know what to do." He gave Alexia a stony stare. "Anything else he said I should know about?"

"No." She looked thoughtful for a moment then said, "It occurred to me we know little about one another, so let's remedy that."

Herleif cocked his head and felt his brows furrow. "And how is that supposed to help us?"

"Knowing lineage, background, abilities, it all matters, and it may give us a clue as to how we proceed with this mission." She moved around the counter to stand by his side. Only she grabbed the tray of food and started to walk to the living room. "Nonia, say goodbye to Herleif and go rest. I'll call you if I need you."

The wolf-dog quickly nuzzled against him before disappearing.

Alexia then called out, "Please grab the mugs and join me on the couch. Might as well get comfortable."

Herleif chuckled and did as asked, carefully handling the mugs with his beefy hands and bringing them to the table in front of the couch. After placing them down and not spilling a drop, he sat, watching Alexia as she picked up her tea. She then curled her legs beneath her bottom and seemed to relax.

"Now, tell me all I need to know about Herleif."

Chapter Six

Alexia watched Herleif, his brow wrinkling once again, and oh, how she wanted to smooth those deep furrows.

She knew little about the many shifters and paranormals, having had minimal contact with any until she'd arrived in New York. Her knowledge came from her mother as well as reading, and even then, accurate information had been limited.

Trolls, for instance. She'd read they were usually large beasts, unappealing in appearance. They were known for their aggression and trickery, and most often solitary creatures living underground or in darkness.

Herleif was certainly large but in no way was his appearance unappealing. He was rather handsome in his brutish way. His hair was wild, and she longed to tangle her fingers it. His skin reminded her of fresh spring grass—one of her favorite colors—and the marks and scars added to his ruggedness. Sure, he'd initially been rude, trying to intimidate her, but she was seeing a civil side to him, and she knew they'd be able to work together.

But the way he spoke about himself, as a troll, made Alexia wonder if there was something wrong with her in finding him physically attractive. When he'd been in human form, it'd been a striking form, but truth be told, she preferred him as his true self.

And when he'd said he was seducing her, had he been teasing? What purpose would that tactic serve? He couldn't have been serious, could he? In wanting her?

She silently chastised herself for doing nearly the same as Herleif had done. While there was no self-loathing, there was self-doubt. Other than being inexperienced, there was nothing wrong with her. She was caring, smart, and attractive. Wasn't she?

Maybe he was teasing and didn't want a human like her. Maybe—

"Why are you scowling?"

Herleif's question snapped her out of her internal discussion. She met his curious gaze and tried to steer the topic back to him. "I'm just wondering why you're delaying in telling me about you. We must trust one another if we're going to work together." She took a sip of her tea while he remained quiet. "If you'd rather I go first..." He still said nothing.

She sighed and began. "I'm Alexia Stavros, born thirty years ago on Karpathos, a Greek Island. I'm an empath with the ability to influence others' mood or feelings. I also guide souls to the afterlife on their destined paths. My mother has the ability, as did her mother, and so on, as did all the women in my family. Apparently, my mother's line can be traced back to the Goddess, Hecate."

"Impressive. Do you think that is why the dream walker came to you? Why you're tasked with this mission?"

"Maybe. Hecate was extremely powerful, but I'm nowhere near her level."

"Maybe you are and don't yet realize." When she remained quiet, he spoke again. "And why are you in New York?"

"My parents—mostly my mother—insisted I experience the *modern* world. She felt I was meant for more than my secluded life on Karpathos. My father's brother, Uncle Nic, works for the SRA, um, the Shifters Relations Agency, and he asked if I'd like to try using my guiding ability on the shifters who fight in the club."

"*Try*? Weren't you already using your skills? You

either do it or you don't. There is no *try*."

She chuckled. "Well, yes, you are correct. I suppose Uncle Nic wanted to see how I'd do in that savage environment. I assured him I could handle it."

"Had you ever been around fighters? Any kind of battle?"

"No," she scoffed. "Life on the Island was rather peaceful. If someone was ill or near the end of their life, I would stay with them until their death then guide their souls. On the occasions I went to the mainland, I'd never known of any activity like that."

"And you said last night was your first in the club?"

"Not in that club, as in The Gin Room, but first in that fight club. Uncle Nic had taken me to The Gin Room in Manhattan close to where he lives and introduced me to shifters there. The co-owner is Oba Izem, a lion shifter whose name literally means king lion. He has the fight club set up similarly. I spent a few weeks there guiding souls before going to the Gotham Point club last night.

"Was there another such as you, before you came?"

"Interestingly enough, no, not that I know of. I presume there was a guide on the other side. It isn't simply left up to—"

"Left up to Fate," he stated at the same time. "Fickle bitch," he mumbled.

"She may be, but such is the way of the cosmos."

He cocked his head and gave Alexia another look. "You believe in that bullshit?"

She gave him a stern look. "It took me some time to come to terms with the thought that all is preordained, and there are still moments when it doesn't sit well with me, so all I'll say is life is a series of choices, and those choices lead to where you are supposed to be."

Herleif snorted before leaning forward to pick up his mug, looking impossibly adorable to Alexia. She tried to stifle her giggle but failed.

"What?" She shook her head, but he persisted. "Do I amuse you?"

"In fact, you do. Now it's your turn."

"I'm still stuck on why your uncle, or anyone thought they needed you? What happened to make them decide your skill was needed with your physical presence rather than allowing a guide to do its work on the other side?"

"I was never told of anything happening, some strange occurrence that alerted them to concerns. Doesn't mean something *wasn't* happening but he felt it wasn't pertinent. I'll have to ask him specifically when he contacts me sometime today." She took a drink, watching Herleif as he remained quiet. Contemplating. "Do you think it could have anything to do with it being Samhain?"

"When the veil thins, and spirits may be able to cross into this realm," he said softly. "It's possible. Did you see other spirits, those who shouldn't have been here?"

Alexia shook her head. "No, and I'd have been able to see them since I have that ability. Even those who try to mask or veil themselves, I can see them." She slanted her head. "You do as well," she stated.

His head snapped up, pinning her with a startled look before quickly calming. "Why do you say that?"

"Pfft, come on, Herleif, don't play me for a fool. You're able to see me when I'm veiled. You can touch Nonia when no one should be able to. And she clearly trusts you, allowing you to be near me. You see the spirits leaving the body when no one else in that club can. Or at least, no one that makes it known they can. You have a power. And maybe you never thought it strange otherwise, but it's an ability most others do not possess."

"I've never known differently, and I learned that, yes, most others do not possess it. I also learned it doesn't matter. So what if I can see spirits leaving the deceased? It has no bearing on who I am or how I live my life."

"Fair enough," she conceded.

He quirked a brow but didn't respond to the topic. Instead he asked, "How long are you staying in New York?"

"I hadn't made any decisions, and now with this going on, well, I certainly can't leave until it's resolved."

"You can do whatever you choose. You aren't bound to help these souls. That is, if you believe what you were told."

Alexia sat up straighter. "You don't believe me?"

"I did not say that, Alexia. What if you weren't told the truth? What if this is some elaborate ruse? A trap?"

"For what purpose?"

"That remains to be seen, now, doesn't it?"

Alexia shook her head as she placed her mug on the table, the tea now cold and bitter. "And why involve both of us? Because I'm sure it does. Nothing like last night happened in the Manhattan club while I'd been there, so I believe you are a factor." She sat back and pulled the fleece throw off the back of the couch to wrap around herself. "Tell me about Herleif Aganarsson. Please."

His nose twitched. "There isn't much to tell. Nothing extraordinary. My family hails from Northern Denmark. I am eighty years of age." Alexia knew her eyes had widened. "Trolls tend to have a good lifespan. My father, who has lived nearly two hundred years, was involved in salt mining and when that went bust, he made the wild move to bring us to America two decades ago."

"Versus remaining in Europe? Wasn't there other work he could have engaged in?"

"Sure, plenty, but my father was impatient and greedy. Not a good combination."

"Which led to this debt you're paying off for him." When his brow rose, Alexia explained. "My uncle knew of this, the reason you're fighting in the club. He said he was going to see what else he could find out about you as well as Evan Hosten."

"Evan?"

"The Lycan you fought and…"

"And killed," he said, hanging his head.

"Herleif, he knew what he was getting into when he stepped into the pit." She leaned closer, touching his arm. He jumped at the contact before his head snapped up, so their gazes locked. "It was a mercy killing and very commendable."

He scoffed and shook his head. Alexia began to withdraw her hand but once again, Herleif surprised her with his speed, grasping her hand with his. The hold was gentle, his hand warm.

Did she see vulnerability in his eyes?

Alexia didn't try to pull away, sensing he needed the contact. "How many do you have in your family?" she asked, wanting to keep him talking.

"Myself, Father, and Mother."

"No extended family?"

"None."

His fingers softly caressed hers and the tender action sent shivers through her. Still, she didn't try to move away from his touch. "Do, or *did* you have a community in Denmark? Other trolls?"

"A few I knew of, no relation, though. My mother tried to form friendships, but my father wanted nothing to do with them. Trolls tend to stick to themselves. My father viewed them as competition. Really, anyone was. As I said, he was greedy."

Alexia shook her head. "Sad he wouldn't want that relationship with his own kind. Have you made friends here?"

"Friends?" He laughed. "No. Trolls don't make friends."

"Why not? You know—or maybe you don't—not everyone views the *Jötnar* as unfriendly or unapproachable. They were a significant presence in our history, many mating with gods."

He grinned. "You think trolls descended from the *Jötnar*?"

"Yes. They were the original giants of the world and revered. Well, by most. Can your family trace their line back generations? Maybe to the days of Odin?"

"Doubtful. I was never told any of that, and it never crossed my mind to ask. Many still believe those tales are merely myth."

"Pfft, you mean humans." Alexia waved away that comment. "It is our history, our lineage. Let the humans, or most of them, believe what they will. There is no denying the presence of the paranormal, even if our kind prefer to limit that knowledge."

"Would you prefer *our kind* make our presence known and fuck the consequences?"

"Herleif, why must you be crude with your language?"

He threw his head back and bellowed with laughter. She startled at first then joined him. "I love your laugh. Shows you aren't always the hardened brute you make yourself out to be."

He quieted and pinned her with an intense stare while his grip on her hand tightened. "You have no idea the brute I am."

Alexia wouldn't be intimidated by him. "Is that so?" She sent a tiny surge of power through her hand, just enough so he'd feel a buzz. "Don't think you know all about me either."

Herleif retained his hold, using his thumb to stroke her knuckles. "I wouldn't dream of underestimating you, Alexia. It's my mission to discover everything about you." He leaned closer while pulling her toward him, so they were inches apart. "How quickly will your skin flush when I see you fully naked?"

Alexia felt her eyes widen as she remained frozen while Herleif brought his mouth to her ear.

"How sweet will your pussy taste." She gasped. He chuckled. "How loudly you'll scream when my cock fills you and brings you ecstasy like you've never felt."

Alexia couldn't contain the whimper that escaped her, and she felt herself pressing closer to this dirty-talking beast she wished would at least kiss her. As for the other things he described, her body trembled at the thought, and it wasn't in fear.

Herleif licked down the column of her neck then worked his way back up to suckle her ear. "Would you like that, Alexia? Would you like for this beast to spread you out and feast on you in every way imaginable?"

"Yes," she moaned without hesitation. But when Herleif stilled, she suddenly wondered if he were simply teasing her. Testing her. She leaned back to look at his face but couldn't discern his thoughts. She used her ability to read his emotions. "You don't believe me."

He frowned but remained silent.

"Why would you say such things, ask me these questions if you weren't prepared for honesty?"

"Because no one wants *me*. The troll."

She dared to gently place her palm against his

cheek and watched his eyes become wary. "Then you've been asking the wrong women." She then laced her fingers into his hair and pulled him to her, so their mouths met. Cautious of the sharp protrusions, Alexia kissed him. She wasn't skilled in this activity at all, but that didn't stop her from doing what she thought felt right.

Herleif stiffened for all of a split-second before he growled and took control. He cradled the back of her head while tipping her chin up, devouring her mouth, and all she felt was bliss.

And, oh gods, did she want more.

VOLUME THREE

Chapter Seven

Herleif wanted desperately to believe her words. His hunger for her grew with every passing minute he remained in her presence. Like a vine twisting around his heart, its hold, tenacious, but not strangling.

Oddly comforting. At least that's how he thought it felt, given he'd never experienced the feeling before. Somehow, he felt at peace. Didn't mean he hadn't liked their snarky banter toward one another. He rather liked the verbal sparring, seeing her strength, her daring, and what she was capable of.

Right now, she was highly capable of fanning the flames of his desire. He feared he'd be too rough, too aggressive. Too much. And he wanted to, *Gods*, how he wanted to ravage her. Own her. But he didn't want to hurt her.

As he started to loosen his hold and gentle the kiss, Alexia whimpered and crawled into his lap, spearing her fingers in his hair and holding him to her. The kiss deepened and he took hold of her hips, grinding her body to his. She moaned into his mouth as she moved her body in time to his movements, and Herleif thought for sure he'd bust right there.

"Alexia," he groaned, pulling away with great effort.

"No, please, don't stop," she pleaded. "Don't tell me why this is a bad idea when it feels so right."

"Be sure of what you're saying, because once I start with you, I will not stop."

She framed his face and locked her eyes on him. "I'm sure."

There was no tremor in her voice, no hesitation. He saw truth in her eyes, and his heart truly skipped a beat at the wonder of her words.

"Then you are mine." He held her ass and stood. Her legs wrapped around him and her gaze never strayed from his.

"I'm yours."

He marched them down the only hallway to where he presumed her bedroom to be. When he found it, he stood short of the threshold and looked past Alexia to take in her space. Earthy colors in various tones of brown, green, orange, and yellow greeted him as the first morning light began to brighten the area. Herleif was surprised yet pleased to see the size of her bed filling the room. His mind conjured wicked thoughts about what he'd do to her in that bed. He looked at her and grinned. "Seems there's plenty of room for the both of us. I hope it's sturdy." He winked.

Her giggle was like fairy music, light and delicate. "It'll hold."

Ducking into the room and stepping to the edge of the bed, he loosened his grip, and she released her legs to stand before him. When she reached for the hem of her shirt, Herleif stopped her and brought her hands to his mouth to kiss. Then he said, "Let me." She nodded and he released her hands to take hold of the material, lifting it off. He took in the beautiful sight of her bare torso and generous breasts. The dark nipples peaked, and he desperately wanted his mouth on them. But first he needed to finish undressing her.

She wore a skirt that tied at her side and hung loosely to her ankles. Her pale bare feet with toenails painted bronze made a stark contrast to his large black boots. Herleif reached for the ties, pulling the ends which allowed the material to fall at her feet. Alexia stepped away from her skirt toward him, pressing her palms against his chest. She ran her fingers down the length of his torso until she reached the hem.

"May I?" she asked as she began to lift the material. But Herleif halted her movement.

"No." She began to frown, and he simply chuckled as he scooped her up, delighting in her squeal. He spread her out on the bed then stood, drinking in the sight of her beautiful body. "You are magnificent." He loved the blush of her cheeks.

Making quick work of shedding his boots and clothes, he watched as Alexia rose onto her elbows to study him, scanning his body. Her perusal brought his cock to attention, and when she met his gaze, there was no mistaking her look of need. And when she licked her lips, Herleif groaned.

"I am going to thoroughly enjoy worshipping every inch of you."

She smiled and drew her legs apart. "What's stopping you?"

The sight of her damp curls and the scent of her arousal had Herleif clenching his hands at his sides. His erection hardened near the point of pain, the tip weeping with moisture.

"Herleif, don't be afraid of hurting me. I'm prepared and know what to expect."

"You may think you're ready, but you aren't yet, and I don't want to hurt you." He fisted his cock and gave it a squeeze. "This is more than most can handle, especially for a virgin pussy."

"Do you expect me to watch you pleasure yourself and leave me wanting?" She trailed a hand down her abdomen and into her curls. "Or shall I join you in the self-pleasure?"

"Woman," he growled.

"You did say you were going to enjoy worshipping every inch of me." She swirled her fingers through her folds, causing herself to gasp. "Will you be true to your word, Herleif?"

Her breathy voice undid him, and he moved quickly, bracing himself above her. "I will. For you." The softening look in her eyes eased the tightness in his chest, dispelling the uneasy feeling of expecting her to change her mind. But her warm smile and welcoming arms cracked his hardened heart, bringing in a breath of life he never thought to feel.

He wouldn't get ahead of himself and think beyond the moment. For now, he'd gladly take whatever she offered.

Leaning down, he molded his mouth to hers, kissing her now with leisure and care. With reverence. She responded in-kind, relaxing beneath him just as she wound her arms around him, splaying her hands against his back. Herleif tried to restrain from pressing his full weight onto Alexia, but she pulled his body to hers, wrapping a leg across the back of his thighs. The feel of her against him, at his mercy, was heady, but he knew he was too much.

Herleif used his strength and speed to hold her and roll, bringing her on top of him. He loved seeing the delight in her eyes as she planted her hands on his chest and sat up. Her fingers traced the many dips and swells along with the scars across his flesh. He watched her closely, looking for any sign of disgust, but he saw only interest. Desire.

While she explored his body, he did the same, tracing her sides until his hands covered her breasts, kneading the generous mounds. Alexia let her head fall back as she moaned, pressing into his touch. She rocked her pelvis into his with a slow and steady rhythm that had her slick pussy sliding across his eager cock.

"Herleif," she moaned.

He tweaked her nipples then flicked the rigid pebbles with a claw, causing her to squeak. When he did it again, she cried out before her gaze met his. He carefully worked his hands beneath her thighs and began to lift her. "You're going to hold onto that frame while I devour that enticing pussy of yours."

"Wh-what? No, you don't—"

"Oh, but I do, Alexia. And I will. Now grab it." He gave her no time as he shifted her body, positioning her sex above his face. Her arms flew forward to find purchase on the metal structure which banged against the wall. He then spread her legs wide and held her aloft as he dragged his tongue through her slit. The instant he tasted her juices he knew he was lost. He was tasting ambrosia. Heaven.

Alexia gasped as he repeated the action. Over and over, he lapped at her pussy, trying to quench his thirst, knowing he never would. Knowing he'd never have enough of her.

He lashed his tongue across her engorged clit, reveling in her noises. Her body seemed to want more as she tried to grind against his face, but he held her at his mercy, delivering unrelenting whips with his tongue. With each strike she shuddered and gasped as her thighs shook in his hands. He wrapped his lips around the bud, suckling, causing her to cry out his name. Her tremors increased as her skin grew dewy with sweat, and he knew she was close to release.

Herleif wanted this pleasure for her. Wanted to be the one to deliver it.

He knew an instant before she came as her body tightened and her breath caught. Then she exploded, dancing frantically, rubbing her pussy against his face as he held her quaking body above him. His cock ached, longing to fill her, knowing it would do so very soon.

Gripping her thighs, he knew for sure he'd leave bruises as if leaving his mark and staking his claim. But they wouldn't be the only marks he left on her. Before this morning ended, she'd know she belonged to no one but him.

He gently lapped at her sex, continuing to flick at her sensitized clit, feeling every twitch and spasm.

"Herleif, please," she pleaded. "I can't … I don't…" Her body went limp, and he sat up, cradling her in his arms as she rode out the orgasm, panting into his neck. "That was … I feel…"

"I'm hoping that was amazing and you feel euphoric."

"Yes." She lightly chuckled. "That's a decent start."

Herleif kissed the side of her head while kneading her shapely ass. "Oh, it's *only* the start. I have much more in store for you." To prove his point, he flexed his erect cock, slapping it against her rear. She started to laugh but it morphed into a squeal when he traced a digit through the crease and carefully teased her hole. Alexia squirmed and tried to move away, but that brought her sex in contact with Herleif's other hand he'd moved between them. He pressed his thumb to her clit as he slowly inserted a finger into her channel, causing her to cry out.

"Easy, relax," he cooed. "You can take it. And you'll take more."

"Herleif," she moaned while pumping her body with the thrusting of his finger. He added a second, stretching her, and her guttural sounds intensified. "So good," she drew out.

"It gets better," he growled, feeling her tighten around his digits. Putting more pressure on her clit, he felt her close to another orgasm. She became wetter, coating his fingers and dripping between them.

It was time.

Pulling his hands away, he earned a gasp then a protest. But he gave her little time to speak as he once again used his speed and power to lift her and notch his erection at her opening. He locked eyes with her, giving her only a second to realize what came next.

"Take me, Alexia, as I claim you as mine."

He drew her body down his length, breaking through her barrier, filling her completely. Her cry turned to a whimper as she clung to him, her pussy surrounding him with exquisite tightness. Herleif wrapped his arms around her, rubbing her back, soothing her while she adjusted to the invasion.

Seconds passed before Alexia leaned back and raised her face to look at him. Although her eyes shone with moisture, they also radiated trust and acceptance. She framed his face and drew him close for a kiss. His heart thundered in his chest as his cock pulsed, eager for movement. Without breaking contact, Herleif maneuvered their bodies so she lay beneath him. Bracing his forearms on either side of her head, he withdrew his cock to the tip, only to slide back inside. He captured her moans, kissing her deeply as he increased his pace, and she matched his movements to perfection. He then placed a hand beneath her ass, changing their angle, sliding in deeper, harder.

"So fucking good," he groaned. "You were made for me, Alexia."

"Yes," she said, her voice breathy. "And you, for me." She wrapped her legs around his waist, meeting his thrusts, grinding herself against his groin.

He felt her tremors, and he couldn't contain his grunts as she gripped him impossibly tighter. "That's it, squeeze me, milk me. Come for me. Come with me." Each word was more difficult than the last as his control began to slip. He couldn't slow his pace, and she didn't seem to mind. Just the opposite—she spurred him on.

"Yes, Herleif," she cried just as she came, clamping down on him like a vise. Her eyes flashed the color of fire, burning with passion before returning to their original emerald. Herleif felt the rush of his orgasm overtake him, and he buried his face in the soft cradle of her shoulder as he hammered into her, spurting his seed. He couldn't stop himself from sinking his teeth into her tender flesh, causing her to cry out and send a rush of power sizzling through him.

Locked together, their orgasms seemed never-ending. And that was fine with Herleif. He could remain inside Alexia until the end of his days, which, God willing, would be a very long time. Eventually their tremors eased, and he removed his mouth from her shoulder, licking the punctures and using a bit of his own power to soothe the wounds. He then withdrew from her, earning a sigh.

"Rest," he whispered then kissed her temple. With more creative maneuvering, Herleif managed to get them beneath the covers, spooning her body as she instantly fell asleep.

Chapter Eight

Alexia felt as if she were floating on water, surrounded by warmth. And when she opened her eyes, that's exactly where she found herself—in her Jacuzzi tub with her and Herleif filling the space.

"How did I not wake before now?" she asked groggily.

Herleif was gently caressing her body, and she realized she felt more energized than she expected.

"I may have persuaded you to rest until your body was ready to wake. I didn't want you feeling any pain, and I also wanted to clean you."

She covered his hands with hers, halting his movements and turning her head to look at him. "Thank you." When he simply nodded, she continued. "For everything. You were ... well, you were wonderful. You made me feel amazing." She turned her head forward. "I wish I had better words to describe it."

Alexia felt Herleif move, his mouth at her ear. "It was exquisite. Intense. Exceptionally marvelous." He ran his tongue down her neck then nuzzled a particularly soft and tender spot.

"Yes," she said and chuckled. "All that and more." Suddenly her hand flew to the base of her neck. "Did you ... did you bite me?" Her fingers found tiny indents.

"Yes. I soothed the bites so you wouldn't feel any residual pain. You will, however, retain my mark."

Alexia shifted her body to face him, her thighs bracketing his. She was completely comfortable with her nakedness, considering what they'd experienced together earlier.

"Are you claiming me as yours, Herleif

Aganarsson?"

His strong hands held her waist, pulling her closer. "I am. I have." He brought her sex against his growing erection. "I told you, you are mine, did I not?"

She smiled as she rested her hands atop his shoulders. "You did. And you are mine." His only response was the brisk nod of his head, and Alexia's pulse beat in double-time.

"Your eyes glowed like fire when you climaxed," Herleif said while gently caressing her lower back.

"Is that so? Well, it was an extraordinary moment. Very powerful." She smiled.

He grinned. "That it was."

She leaned forward, looping her arms around his neck to kiss him, then drew back. "How am I only now realizing you morphed your mouth when kissing me? You made these disappear." She ran a finger across an extended tooth, pressing against the sharp point and causing a droplet of blood to well.

Herleif took her finger, inserting it into his mouth to suck off the crimson liquid. "Yes, I did. Other than intentionally biting you, I did not want to harm you with my tusks."

"Tusks," she murmured. "Not canines?"

He shrugged. "Some call them that."

"Herleif? You don't have to alter who you are or what you have. I want it all." She began kissing him, working around his teeth and taking her time to thoroughly enjoy this moment.

But just as she began to grind herself against him, hoping for another joining, her phone blared, startling them.

"What is that godawful sound?" Herleif growled.

"My phone. It's my uncle."

Herleif pulled her even closer. "Ignore him." He

tried resuming the kiss, but she averted her face.

"I cannot. He'll persist until I answer, or he'll be at my door in less than thirty minutes."

"Plenty of time for me to fuck you." He grinned.

She gave him a playful glare even as she punched his shoulder. "Enough." After a quick peck on the lips, she moved away and rose out of the tub. Wrapping herself in a towel, she stared down at his glorious body. "Might as well dry and dress. No doubt he's called to tell me he's on his way over."

Alexia turned away to go to her bedroom, grinning at Herleif's startled look. She heard him splashing about before stomping toward her. She quickly dried herself and began to pull clothes out when he arrived in her room.

"Do you wish me to leave?"

"No. Why would I want that?" Watching his face screw up in confusion, she marched to him. "Herleif, if I have to tell you one more time that I want you here, and that I am not ashamed of wanting you, you're going to feel your ass zapped again. Is that clear?"

A slow grin spread across his handsome face as he palmed a cheek. "That is clear." He leaned down to give her a gentle kiss. When he pulled back, she smiled at him before spinning to get dressed. She received a swat on her rear, causing her to yelp and look back at him.

"I like you feisty." He winked.

She scoffed and rolled her eyes as she resumed her task. "Then dry my floor."

"Gladly," he said and chuckled.

Moments later, dressed and the floor cleaned, they were back in the living room. She noticed the tray of food and mugs of tea were nowhere to be seen. She turned to Herleif. "Thank you for tidying up." He merely smiled and dipped his head. Picking up her phone, they listened to her uncle's message.

"I have news and am on my way over."

Simple and direct.

Alexia put down her phone and headed to the kitchen. "Time for more food and tea." She grinned.

Fifteen minutes later, she was opening the door to her Uncle Nic, welcoming him in, and taking his coat. He stopped short when Herleif stood, apparently ready to greet him. "You're…"

"Herleif Aganarsson," Herleif said, offering his hand. Uncle Nic hesitated a second before grasping it to shake. He then looked at Alexia in question.

"Sit, please," she said, indicating to the chair flanking the couch. She then went to Herleif's side, looping her arm with his and pulling him down on the couch beside her. "Seems we both have news to share. Help yourself." She nodded to the food and drink while getting a mug and offering it to Herleif before grabbing one for herself.

"It would seem so," her uncle said. He then lifted a cup and took a drink, never taking his eyes off Herleif.

"Uncle Nic, no need to be wary or awkward. You can speak freely, and you can trust Herleif." She looked at her … lover? While she wasn't going to divulge details, she also wasn't going to hide the fact that they were more than … friends? Gah, it was all so new, and Alexia wasn't sure how to navigate this budding relationship. "He came to me this morning regarding a mutual visitor we both had."

"Visitor?"

"A dream walker on behalf of Fate," Alexia began then detailed her experience and conversation. Herleif added his as well with Uncle Nic interjecting at times with questions for clarification.

"And this messenger deemed you two would

work together," he stated.

"Yes," Alexia answered. "He said there is more to Herleif than even he realizes." She faced her troll. "And that he would not forsake me."

"Never," Herleif whispered to her. "As for some hidden power or talent, he must be mistaken."

"I suppose we'll see."

Alexia turned back to her uncle who was watching their interaction with curiosity but remained quiet about it. "A fucking soul collector," he mumbled with disgust.

"Were you aware of this happening or has it happened before?" Herleif asked.

"No, I was not aware of it happening now or ever, but it could explain recent concerns with the fights."

"What concerns?" Alexia asked. "And which fights? Gotham Point or other locations?"

"*All* locations."

"The Lycan said, 'Don't let him take my soul. Him,'" Herleif restated. "Who is *him* and is he somehow coercing shifters? If so, how? It was clear to me that Evan was fighting for his life in a way many others did not, and he did not want this soul collector to win."

"I learned that Evan Hosten was a pack leader, fighting in place of his son. But I haven't been able to find out *why* he fought instead of the son. And now the son has disappeared without a trace."

"Where is his pack from?" Alexia asked. "How does no one have any information on his whereabouts?"

Her Uncle Nic sighed. "He is one shifter among thousands in New York City alone. Tens of thousands in the entire state. Their pack is located upstate near the Canadian border. I've sent an agent to investigate."

"And what of these concerns in all The Gin Room locations?" Herleif asked.

VOLUME THREE

Uncle Nic faced him. "Increased activity, more fights. Curiously enough, the majority of them involving Lycan. And they've been more aggressive fights at that. All within the past week. Of course, the spectators and bidders aren't going to complain, but my agents have taken notice."

"Leading up to Samhain, which is tonight," Alexia said.

"Did Evan ascend?" Alexia's uncle asked of her.

"He did. But when he did, he passed through me versus me simply guiding him, showing him the way. And somehow, a portion of his essence, his energy, remained with me."

"What?" Both men shouted at the same time.

"Why did you not say something to me?" her uncle said.

"Or me?" Herleif groused.

"Because at the time we spoke, Uncle, I was unaware. It was only when I teleported back to my apartment after my first encounter with Herleif, did I realize it hadn't taken as much energy as previous times." She then turned to Herleif. "And, because the subject didn't come up." She cleared her throat, knowing she was blushing as she thought about what occurred during their recent encounter. "Now, whether that were to happen again, I cannot say. The only way to know is to return to the fights—the pit, to be exact—and guide the next soul."

"No," both men bellowed again.

Alexia felt herself scowl. "Neither of you can tell me *no*. It is what I do. It may even be the way to locate this soul collector. I have the ability to follow the soul, and I've no doubt the collector will be active tonight. Maybe even now." She looked at her uncle. "Are there fights taking place now?"

"Yes. Usually, they'd only occur at night, but as I

said, activity has increased and now they're happening continuously."

Alexia was on her feet, looking between the two men. "Then we must go. Now."

"Alexia," Herleif began as he took her hand in his. "Sit, eat. You need your strength. We ate nothing this morning."

A quick glance at her uncle, and Alexia saw his brow quirk in question. She ignored it and sat, grabbing bites of the food and sipping her tea. "I wonder how long this soul collector has been active? And how he—if he is indeed a *he*—is getting away with it?" She looked at Herleif then at her uncle. "Mother never spoke to me about someone she or others before her had to answer to. Throughout history, there were and still are many psychopomps who—"

"I'm sorry, what?" Herleif interrupted. "Psychopomps?"

"It's the term that describes a guider of souls. As I said, there were many, like Hecate herself, Charon, the ferryman, Anubis, the Egyptian god."

"Valkyries," he said softly.

"Exactly. Every religion, culture, aspect of humankind had their version of a soul guider. I am but one among an indeterminate amount. I never questioned my ability, and before last night, I was never visited by an entity regarding my skill or mission." She took another sip of tea. "Why now is Fate sending someone to us, telling us we are to stop him?"

"I wish I had answers to those questions," Herleif said.

"*Ki ego*," her uncle mumbled. He then popped his head up and said, "Apologies, slipping back to my Greek. Me too, I said." He looked at Herleif. "If you don't mind telling me, what are your powers? Other than strength.

Are you a shape-shifter?"

"I am, only to human form." Without any effort at all, he shifted to his Viking then back again, causing Alexia's uncle to startle.

"Wow, okay, impressive."

Herleif simply chuckled. "And yes, I have my strength and speed, but I also have a limited ability to heal and influence others in subtle ways."

"Like ensuring I rested," Alexia said. Herleif only nodded. "I too can influence most. But not you. I had to zap you to get my point across."

They chuckled together for a moment until Alexia realized her uncle was staring again. She looped an arm around one of Herleif's. "You may have surmised, Herleif and I are very comfortable with one another. In fact," she glanced at Herleif before facing her uncle again, "we are lovers." She felt the subtle tensing of Herleif but gave him a reassuring squeeze.

"Oh, I see." His gaze toggled between the two. "That was quick."

Alexia smiled up at Herleif and whispered, "It was Fate." She winked, receiving an endearing smile from her troll. Her heart fluttered at the thought and at the feeling of rightness.

"Well then," her uncle started, "what's your plan?"

"We go to the fights," Alexia said. "And we go now. We need to get a sense of any unease or the presence of this soul collector. If need be, as I said, I will follow a soul and see where, or to whom, it leads."

"I do not like this," Herleif stated. When Alexia started to protest, he held up a hand. "I realize this is your journey and you are fully capable, but something feels off. And don't ask me to expand because I cannot. It's just a feeling."

"Then we will be vigilant, and we will stay together."

"Are you able to call upon Nonia anywhere, anytime?" Herleif asked.

"I can. She's never failed me."

He nodded and stood, holding out his hand for her. "Then we go."

VOLUME THREE

Chapter Nine

Herleif walked into The Gin Room with a churning in his gut. More than a niggling that something about this entire situation wasn't what it appeared to be. He wished he knew why, wished he could find a reason for the feeling, but nothing coalesced in his mind. Lately he'd been troubled in sleep, restless with dreams, but again, nothing remained in his memories. Nothing other than the recent visit from Fate's messenger, and that had been troubling enough.

Not wanting to burden Alexia with his concerns, he kept it to himself, allowing her to concentrate on what she needed to do.

Herleif felt an instant calm as a warmth started in his hand, spread up his arm, and over his torso. He looked down at Alexia, knowing she was trying to soothe him. He also saw the questions in her eyes and a tight smile on her otherwise beautiful face.

"What is it? What's wrong?"

He stopped short when he heard her voice in his head.

"You heard me?"

He gave a brisk nod before leading them to a darkened corner. "How are you doing that?"

"I honestly don't know, given you seemed immune to my influence. I only thought to give it a try." She remained quiet a moment as if thinking then opened her mouth but closed it again without saying a word.

"Tell me your thoughts, Alexia."

"Maybe since our joining, since you bit me … could that have altered something between us? Formed a bond?"

"Like vampires?" She gave a careless shrug.

"Alexia." Her bright eyes told him she'd heard him in her mind. *"I rather like this and the idea we are ... bonding."*

She smiled broadly as she placed a hand on his chest. *"I do as well."*

Before either could say more, a ruckus was heard in the corridor leading down to the fight club. Herleif watched Dax, the man he knew as a panther shifter, sprint in that direction.

"Let's go," Alexia said, pulling him in that direction. "Must be serious if Dax is headed down there."

They moved through the growing crowd, making their way toward the steps when they saw two men fighting and Dax trying to break it up. Another joined the melee, and they all managed to tumble down the stairs, crashing to the floor below. Herleif removed himself from Alexia's grasp and jumped down the stairwell. He saw Dax had shifted and was fighting a wolf while not far away were two more wolves biting and clawing one another.

Spectators began to form a semicircle around the fighters even as the two other arenas carried on as if nothing unusual was happening. Herleif shoved his way past the onlookers to grab ahold of the Lycan ready to jump Dax. Once held firmly, he commanded, "Shift."

Herleif found himself holding a burly man, but he was no match for troll strength. The guy continued to yell, fighting his restraint so that Herleif had no choice but to knock him out and let him crumple to the floor. Dax shifted back to human form just as Alexia reached Herleif's side.

The roar of the crowd drew their attention to the other two Lycan. The beasts, bloodied and ragged, were now circling one another, growling and snarling. No one seemed to mind that a third arena was now open for bets.

"Who are these wolves and why were they

fighting above?" Herleif asked of Dax.

The panther shifter shook his head. "I have no idea who they are or what caused their fight. More and more Lycan have been showing up, causing trouble. Tonight, of all nights, we're packed to the rafters, and more than half the patrons are wolves. We've had to turn many away, and I'm sure you saw the waiting line out the door."

"Uncle said more of the fights lately have involved wolves. Are the other clubs experiencing the same?"

Dax nodded. "Yes, in fact, it was Tor, from Oba's Manhattan club, who contacted us to give us a heads-up. They had their share of instigators as well, said a group talked about making the rounds to all the clubs' parties before heading to the fights. So, we brought in even more help for the evening than we had already planned. Fucking Halloween." He swiped a hand through his hair and sighed.

Alexia stepped to him, touching his arm. "Dax, you're bleeding. That's a nasty looking gash." Dax turned his arm and cursed. "Go get that cleaned up."

He looked at Alexia and grinned. "Yes, ma'am. Guess that's another raincheck on the drinks." Looking at Herleif, he asked, "Are you here to fight?"

"Hadn't planned on it." He looked at Alexia then back at Dax. "We have another mission tonight." He wrapped his arm around Alexia's waist, drawing her closer.

"Okay then, well, good luck. Catch up later."

Herleif nodded then watched the man walk away before looking at Alexia again. "Shall we?" He indicated toward the wolves who were now locked together as one held the other's throat. "Doesn't look like it's going to take long."

Her eyes held sadness, and Herleif wished he could spare her the grief she felt. Yet he knew she was strong and didn't need him sheltering her from experiences she'd dealt with before and would no doubt deal with again.

Alexia gave a nod and marched closer. They came to the edge of the crowd when howls split the air–one clearly in misery, the other louder, signaling victory. One of the wolves stood over the other, flesh hanging from his jowls as blood pooled around the prone wolf on the ground whose throat had been ripped out. The victor snarled and slung the trophy from his mouth, causing viewers to scream as they tried to avoid being hit. The wolf then seemed to lock eyes on its next victim, a woman who stood next to Herleif.

"Watch for the soul," Herleif said to Alexia. "I'll take care of this fucker."

She looked as if she wanted to protest, but Herleif turned away and focused on the bloodthirsty Lycan. "Ready to face a worthy opponent?" He taunted, gaining the wolf's attention. "That's right, let's go. Unless you're too much of a pussy to fight me."

His words had the desired effect when the wolf bared his teeth and leapt at Herleif. He easily skirted the attack while landing a punishing blow to the animal's skull, sending him crashing to the ground, whimpering. Herleif then caught sight of the expected light ascending from the first fallen wolf. Alexia stood over the creature as his soul wound its way toward her.

As with the first time he witnessed it, Herleif wanted to warn her, protect her, but knew he shouldn't. Wouldn't. He watched as Alexia absorbed the light, her eyes flashing as bright as the sun. Just as the soul began to spiral upward, a piercing screech jerked his attention to the wolf he thought he'd only knocked out. But an eerie light of murky gray oozed out of the body and blasted toward Alexia.

"No!" Herleif bellowed as he threw himself between it and his lover, wrapping his arms around his woman to shield her from the assault. Alexia tensed and screamed as he absorbed the impact of what felt like a bullet train slamming into him. The underground disappeared as they barreled through time and space, feeling as if they were being sucked through a vacuum.

They came to an abrupt halt, the sudden impact jarring their bodies, causing both to grunt. They lay in a tangle for a moment, getting their bearings before rising and remaining at each other's side. Except for a hazy amber glow in the distance, darkness permeated the space around them, and the smell of sulfur filled the air.

"What the hell?" Herleif murmured.

"Exactly," Alexia said as she looked up at him. "What happened? I remember the wolf's soul seeking me out then you grabbing ahold of me."

She produced the blue light in her palm and held it high, illuminating the space. A rocky floor lay beneath their feet and stone walls dripping with brown sludge rose on both sides, creating a corridor as wide as a city street.

"The wolf I thought I knocked out apparently died. Only his soul that rose from the body wasn't a light, it was more like … like that." He pointed to the wall. "Some gray glob of muck." He looked at Alexia. "But it targeted you."

"What? Me? Why?"

Herleif shook his head. "I don't know, but it shot straight for you with surprising speed. I only meant to shield you. It must have propelled us, here." He waved his hand about. "Wherever here is."

"We're in a realm in the Underworld, and you had

nothing to do with getting us here. It was the demented soul of the wolf you killed. I feel it." The blue light changed to a fireball just as whispers were heard echoing throughout the cavern. Soft at first, they grew louder until Herleif thought it almost unbearable.

"Souls?" he questioned in a raised voice.

"Yes. Many belong here. Others do not." Nonia suddenly appeared at Alexia's side, growling low, and the voices began to quiet. Herleif watched Alexia place her hand on the wolf-dog's head, massaging through the fur, comforting her.

"And what of the other soul, did it ascend?"

"It did not. It's trapped among those here that do not belong."

"Who is doing this?" he practically shouted. Nonia's growling grew louder just before a voice crackled around them.

"I'm so glad you asked."

A giant wolf stepped out of the darkness, walking upright like a human. Ghostly apparitions trailed closely behind as torches suddenly came to life along the rocky walls. Alexia extinguished her fireball, but Herleif sensed she remained poised for anything. The figure was as tall as Herleif with the mangiest coating he'd ever seen. Black eyes gleamed with dark delight and jowls dripped with thick saliva while smiling with what could only be described as an evil grin.

"Fenrir?" Alexia said in shock. Nonia barked, causing the apparitions to cower, while the wolf merely laughed, instantly grating on Herleif's nerves.

"None other, my dear. Welcome to my realm." He raised his arms in a flourish. "I hope you're prepared to stay a while."

Chapter Ten

Like hell, Alexia thought but surely wasn't going to voice that. The beast would never let her live that little pun down.

"Are you fucking kidding me?" Herleif said.

"She is not, my handsome troll," Fenrir said.

Herleif practically growled. "I am not your *anything*."

This only seemed to delight the wolf as he threw his head back and laughed. "Oh, but you are going to be a fun addition to my realm."

Herleif started forward, fists bunched, until Alexia placed her hand on his arm, stepping closer to his side. When Fenrir began approaching with confidence, making his way directly to her, Herleif put himself in between her and the beast.

"Ah, is someone being territorial?" His tongue whipped out to lick his snout while he rubbed his paws together as if they were hands.

"Touch her and die." Those gruff words from her lover sent more than warmth through her entire being, confirming the bond forming between them. It was fortification.

Fenrir began to circle them as Alexia and Herleif countered, never letting him out of their site. He kept his distance. For now. But Alexia wouldn't be fooled by his calm demeanor, knowing this beast was a trickster of the highest order. His father was Loki, after all, the most famous *Jötnar* in their history.

"What are you up to, Fenrir?" Alexia asked.

"Isn't it obvious, my beauty?" Herleif growled once again but Fenrir wasn't fazed in the least. He twisted his body, indicating toward the apparitions behind him. "I'm building my army."

"You're the soul collector," she stated. Then asked, "Army? For what purpose?"

The beast tsked and shook his head as if disappointed. "Don't be obtuse, my dear. The only purpose for an army is battle and a war is coming. Sooner than you might think."

"Whose war? Yours?" Herleif scoffed. "And spirits are your soldiers? Good luck with that."

"Oh, I won't need luck. I have all I will need right here."

His gaze never strayed from Alexia, and she shivered at the dark feeling that overcame her. Nonia pushed against her leg while rumbling a warning as Herleif stepped as close as he could, brushing his body to hers. Alexia brought up a hand, calling upon her magic and producing a blue light darker than any she'd ever conjured.

Fenrir seemed to shiver. "Mmm, how I love your show of strength. Sadly, it does *you* no good." He drolled as if bored. "This is *my* realm, and my magic, my strength is the only one that will prevail. And with it, I will finally have my revenge and return the world to the old order. When wildness reigned and chaos ruled!" He raised his hands, and the souls drew closer to him, chanting his name.

"Ragnarok wasn't enough for you?" Alexia asked. "You were killed once, and you'll be defeated again. This time, for good."

The beast laughed. "Oh, such sweet innocence. That purity of power will certainly be of use. To me."

Alexia knew to react, pushing out her power to erect a protective shield around herself, Herleif, and Nonia. The force of Fenrir's magic thrown at them shook the cavern, but her shield held.

"By the gods," Herleif mumbled. "Can you hold him off?"

"I will do my best, but I do not know his strength. He's been feeding off the souls, collecting their essence. And for how long? Your guess is as good as mine."

"Can I move in and out of your shield?"

Alexia startled and snapped her gaze to Herleif. "Do not try, Herleif. His power is considerable, that I can feel. Even your speed and strength may be no match for him."

"I must try something."

Just as he spoke, the air around them sizzled and quaked as Fenrir roared, increasing his efforts and causing her shield to ripple. The souls condensed behind him, screeching. Nonia howled then broke through the barrier, charging.

"No!" Alexia yelled, ready to follow.

"Hold!" Herleif yelled as he threw up his arm to block her. "Look!"

A dozen more wolf-dogs materialized, followed by a dozen more, their manes aflame as they too charged the souls. They swiped, lashed out, and jumped through the spirits, causing them to dissipate. This only enraged Fenrir and he turned his attention to the animals. Propelling spheres of power at them, the dogs were knocked back, whining or disappearing altogether, only to have others take their place.

Alexia watched as Nonia circled, preparing to attack. She couldn't stand by and do nothing, putting the burden on the wolf-dogs. Before Herleif could stop her, she dropped the shield and threw all her power into Fenrir, taking advantage of his back to them. He stumbled just as Nonia pounced, but the attack only seemed to annoy Fenrir as he batted the wolf-dog away, sending her crashing against the rock wall.

"Nonia!"

Herleif shouted for her, but Alexia moved to her companion's side, sending a wave of healing magic across her. She watched as Herleif sped toward Fenrir, pummeling him with all his might. The giant wolf was stunned but quickly recovered, battling Herleif with both power and punches. Round and round they went, exchanging blows until Fenrir began to gain the upper hand. With another blast of his magic, he sent Herleif flying right into the center of the souls. They scattered but their focus remained on her troll. She had no idea what they could do to him, given Fenrir's influence over them, but she took no chances.

Alexia threw up a protective shield around him, giving him time to recover, knowing he'd charge out again when ready. She watched as the wolf-dogs continued to attack, dispatching the spirits, then turned to face her foe.

"You only delay the inevitable," Fenrir said, his paws flexing as his mouth dripped with even more disgusting spittle. "Cease your fruitless efforts or prepare to witness the agony I can inflict."

Alexia cocked her head, staring at him. "Tell me, how did you coerce the shifters to fight—to the death, no less—in order for you to take their souls? If you're so powerful, why not simply, take their souls?" She tapped her finger against her chin in a mocking manner, delighting in Fenrir's confusion at the sudden change in tactics. Snapping her fingers, Alexia smirked. "Oh, that's right. Because you don't *have* that kind of power." She dropped her hands but prepared to call her own power, knowing she was inciting the beast.

Fenrir reared back, puffing his chest like a proud peacock as he snorted and sneered. "They are Lycan! It is their duty to sacrifice to me!"

"Huh. And did you falsely promise them glory in the afterlife, all the while gloating, knowing you'd take their souls and discard them like empty husks?"

Fenrir roared, once again shaking the walls, causing debris to tumble to the floor. The torches brightened and the spirits wailed. Alexia glanced beyond the beast to see Herleif stand, remaining within her shield.

"What are you doing, woman?"

"Trust me."

"Alexia..."

Before more could be said, the monstrous wolf pinned her with a steely gaze as he thrust magic in her direction. Alexia teleported across the cavern to stand just beyond the gathering of spirits. Nonia stood at her side as the other wolf-dogs formed a semicircle around her. Fenrir spun, bellowing his anger.

"You think to evade me but you're no match for my power!" He sucked up soul after soul, their murky essence flowing into him. His eyes glowed like red-hot lava as his mangy fur grew longer, thicker like dead tangled weeds. Claws extended from his paws, and he threw his arms up as if in victory. Pinning Alexia with a demented stare, he snarled. "You will be mine!"

Reacting a millisecond too late, Alexia was forcibly drawn to the beast, caught in his putrid embrace. "Yes," he purred while licking her cheek, and it took all her control not to puke.

"Get your fucking paws off her!" Herleif shouted as he raced toward them, only to be tossed back once again by Fenrir's magic. Alexia managed to contain her cry of concern, not wanting the beast to inflict any more damage to her troll.

"That's better." Fenrir pierced her with his inky gaze. "When I syphon your power, I will rule. And I will keep you at my side, fucking you, watching your body swell with my seed." He trailed a paw down her body and across her belly before cupping her sex. "You will build my brood."

"I would rather die a million deaths," she gritted out.

Alexia then called upon her magic to dislodge herself, only to get knocked back from the combined force of her and Fenrir's power as he countered her attempt. The wolf-dogs howled as half disappeared. Dazed but not defeated, she stood just as Herleif and Nonia made it to her side.

"Shield yourself!" he shouted as her wolf-dog whined.

She knocked away another wave of power and listened as the souls began to moan. *"I have a plan!"*

Herleif managed to dodge a blast but wasn't so lucky with another as he was launched against the wall at their backs. *"Then execute it! I won't lose you!"*

"Nor I, you!"

Alexia screamed like a banshee as she sent a blast toward Fenrir, sending him tumbling like a ragdoll across the rocky ground. He regained his feet and smiled. "Impressive. But it still won't be enough to save you."

Just as he prepared for another attack, Alexia raised her hands and surrounded herself with white light. *"Ela so menna! Xefygete apo to kako! T eleutheroso tis psyches sas!"*

She called upon everything within her, everything from her Greek ancestors, beseeching the souls to come to her and escape the evil. Promising to free their souls.

The spirits' tone clearly changed to one less mournful as they transformed to a brighter essence, rushing toward her with urgency. She braced for the impact of power she knew she'd absorb while guiding them to their destined place in the afterlife.

Alexia barely registered the fury of Fenrir or the alarmed shout from Herleif. She held the power around her as her heart threatened to explode while every cell in her body became electrified. But she held true to her promise, completing what she'd always been tasked to do.

Alexia freed every soul from Fenrir's hold.

She then collapsed as her world went black.

VOLUME THREE

Chapter Eleven

Herleif caught Alexia before she hit the ground, her body trembling yet burning like fire. Her skin was flush and slick with sweat. Nonia altered between crying and howling, but Herleif had no commands, no words to console the wolf-dog. He paid no heed to Fenrir who lay collapsed in a heap, moaning pitifully.

Alexia was his priority.

A quick glance around indicated every soul must have ascended since no apparitions remained. Herleif cradled Alexia in his arms murmuring to her, coaxing her to wake, but she didn't respond.

"Alexia, my love, you must wake. Only you can get us out of here. You don't want to remain trapped in this purgatory, or wherever in hell it is, do you?"

He smoothed the damp hair away from her face as she continued to burn. He'd never felt so helpless, not knowing what to do. There was no chance he'd find water in this godforsaken place, was there?

Herleif looked at the cowering beast who seemed to shrivel even more before his eyes. "Tell me how to get out of here!"

Fenrir attempted to laugh but instead produced a horrific cough that brought forth blood and phlegm. "As if … I'd assist you," he said, struggling to speak as more coughing overtook him. "You both deserve to rot."

"I will end you for good!" Herleif roared. Nonia growled and started to approach the beast, but Herleif stopped her. "That scum isn't worth it," he sighed, knowing he'd get nothing from the despicable monster.

"Alexia, please, find your strength, it's there. Return to me," he pleaded, uncaring how desperate he sounded. Uncaring there was a tremor in his voice.

"We've only found one another. It can't end like this."

"Oh, but it can," Fenrir groaned low. "And it will." He managed to giggle like a lunatic.

Herleif's head snapped up as he retorted with a warrior's cry. Although he didn't want to release her, he carefully placed Alexia on the ground before stalking to the wolf. "Your days are over." He proceeded to take out his aggressions on the foul creature, stomping and pummeling his body until only broken bones within a bloody heap remained. A dark gray mist rose from the pile, dispersing toward the ceiling before it vanished altogether.

Throwing his head back, he bellowed his fury and despair into the void. "If there is a God, hear my words! Bring Alexia back! She deserves her life, with or without me! I'll pay any price! *Ved gudene, spar henne!*" By the gods, spare her, he beseeched.

"You know the price."

Herleif stilled at the disembodied voice he knew. The dream walker. His gut clenched at the memory of all that had been told to him. Details he'd withheld from Alexia. Details he'd hoped wouldn't come to fruition.

He hung his head as Nonia came beside him, whining as she rubbed her body against his legs, offering her support. Herleif sank his fingers into her coat in a selfish move to soothe himself, knowing the task that lay ahead would gut him. Nonia raised her head to look up at him as if questioning. Or possibly offering help.

Giving her a brisk rub, he withdrew his hand from her soft coat to clench his fist at his side. "Return to your mistress. I'm going to save her and send her back." Nonia gave another whine then a yip before padding to Alexia and resting at her side. Herleif gazed at the pair, noticing Alexia's body appeared calm, her color almost returned to normal as if simply resting. Oh, how he longed to lay with her and never leave her. He wished he could experience once again the love Alexia had so willingly given to him.

He turned away before he changed his mind. She deserved to live a life for which she was meant.

When first visited by Fate's messenger, he was told he'd have to make a difficult choice for those he loved. That his heart would guide him in making the decision.

If there was a sacrifice to be made in order to save Alexia, he'd gladly make it.

"Show me."

A vision appeared, causing Herleif to bristle, every muscle in his body clenching. His father, Agnar, was shown speaking with a man as money changed hands—money being given to Agnar. Vision after vision flashed before Herleif as his father seemed to conduct business with many, the money beginning to flow both ways. He heard none of the conversations, but with each vision, his father appeared to look younger and younger.

"What the fuck is this?" Herleif murmured.

The next vision was Agnar and Herleif's mother, Ida, who looked tired and worn down. They were at their home in Denmark and seemed to be arguing, his father becoming so enraged he struck his wife. Ida took the blow without cowering, without shedding a tear. She simply looked at her husband with sadness and disappointment before turning and walking away.

Herleif fisted his hands and clenched his teeth until his jaw throbbed. "Why am I being shown this? What does this have to do with Alexia?"

"A choice must be made."

"What choice?" he yelled.

Suddenly, Herleif saw another figure with his father, a man who looked like a younger version of Evan

Hosten, the Lycan who died at the hands of Herleif in the pit.

"What are you about, Father?"

The scene became clearer, and Herleif recognized the waterfront area beyond the Gotham Point Gin Room.

"How…" Herleif quieted when he was able to hear the conversation this time.

"Find the shifters, especially the Lycan," Hosten said, handing Agnar a giant wad of money. "Entice them to fight with the promise of an even greater reward. Send them to the Manhattan or Gotham Point clubs." He nodded his head in the direction of the nearby club where Herleif had been fighting.

"Just be sure you don't forget about *my* reward," Agnar said as he pocketed the cash.

"Oh, not to worry. This won't go unnoticed." Hosten smirked.

Agnar simply snorted before turning away. He shifted into human form and took to the streets. Hosten remained in the shadows until a few moments later, a figure materialized, similar to how Herleif viewed Alexia when veiled.

Fenrir.

Herleif growled as he listened to more conversation.

"He is doing my bidding?" the beast asked.

"Of course, the greedy bastard," Hosten replied.

"And what of Alexia? You've seen her?"

"Yes, she's toured the clubs and is expected at the Gotham Point fight club tomorrow. I take it her power is immense?"

Fenrir cackled. "Oh, you have no idea. I've watched her lineage for generations, and she is the strongest of all. She will serve me well. No longer will I have to wait until Samhain, until the veils thins. Soon I'll be able to traverse the realms as I please." He then stared at Hosten. "Continue your work and remain elusive."

The young Lycan nodded. "Will do." He walked away without a backward glance.

"Soon, my beauty, you will be mine and the world will be ours." Fenrir's image shimmered before disappearing altogether.

Herleif vibrated with rage, digging his claws into his palms until he bled. Obviously, this meeting occurred two nights ago and no doubt Agnar remained in the city. And of course, he wasn't going to chance getting in touch with his own son and possibly ruin his mission for the unholy beast. The beast his father had no idea no longer lived.

"*Father!*" he roared. "You traitorous fool!"

"He has let his greed consume him, becoming a contributor to this imbalance. You have defeated the beast, but unfortunately your father is due a penalty."

"He's due more than that," Herleif grumbled. "What must I do?" Herleif questioned, already knowing in his gut the choice he would be faced with. "And what of Hosten? He betrayed his own father, did he not?"

"He did and his kind have already dealt with him. Now it is time for you to deal with your father."

"And how will that save Alexia?" Herleif received no answer as the wind suddenly stirred in the stifling cavern as air rushed about, lifting Herleif's hair. A pop echoed before Agnar appeared, standing ten feet from his son. He spun, looking around in confusion before facing Herleif again, his eyes widening.

"How did I get here? What have you done?" He spotted the mangled pile of what was once Fenrir, blood seeping into the cracks of the rocky floor. "What is that?"

"That is the beast you conspired with. The one who fed your greed, never intending to do more for you,

213

other than drain your soul."

"What do you mean? I never conspired with a beast. I—" Agnar clamped his mouth shut, scowling.

"Say it, Father. Tell me how you were brought back to the States. Tell me how you were given funds after funds to not only entice shifters to fight, but to also pad your greedy pockets."

Agnar's eyes widened for a split second before narrowing. "How do you know of this?"

With each passing moment, Agnar began to revert to his aged form, losing whatever vitality he was spelled with. Was that because of Fenrir's demise?

"So, you do not deny my accusations? You admit to your abhorrent acts?"

"There is nothing abhorrent about wanting more, about wanting a good life with the ability to do anything I wish."

Herleif threw his head back and laughed. He then pinned his father with a hardened stare. "No, there is nothing wrong with wanting a good life, but you had that. A good wife and partner. An obedient son willing to sacrifice time from his life to pay your debt, all because I did not want your life ended. But that wasn't good enough, was it? You have forsaken your wife, and you have betrayed your son."

"How have I betrayed you?" He waved his hand carelessly at Herleif. "You still live and breathe, do you not? You still have the ability to fight and be rewarded handsomely, do you not?"

"Yes, Father, I still live and breathe, and I may have the ability to fight, but I'm done with that. I will never step foot in any fight club again."

"Then join me. I've been promised riches! I—"

"You will get nothing!" Herleif fisted his hands. "You. Were. Duped. Played a fool." He pointed down at what remained of Fenrir. "This is the beast behind the false promises you were given. Behind any fleeting magic that even now no longer has power. Do you not feel it? Feel the spell waning?"

Agnar suddenly stooped as if his back couldn't hold his weight. He lifted his hands and watched them bend, contort, and wrinkle before his eyes. He looked at his son with fear.

"What is this trickery? What is happening?"

"It's not trickery, Father, it's the truth. The truth of who you are: an old troll who must now pay for his sins."

"No!"

"You will! Your actions contributed to lost lives." Herleif pointed to where Alexia lay, Nonia by her side, growling low as the wolf-dog stared in Agnar's direction. "I had just begun to discover love." The realization of that hit Herleif like a sucker punch to the gut. "She accepted me for me," Herleif said softly. "And now I may never know what it's like to live out the remainder of my days with someone who cares for me. With someone I came to care about in no time at all."

Agnar sank to his knees, his face even more aged and gaunt. "It can't end like this. It's not supposed to be like this," he whined. "It's not fair."

"Fair? You have the audacity to question what is not fair?" Herleif bellowed as he marched up to his father. "Look at her! Look at the woman I love who may have paid with her life to spare someone like you, so that you may live!"

When Agnar didn't lift his head to look at Alexia, Herleif stomped to him, bending down to grab his jaw and twist his head, so he had no choice but to see. "She had a purpose and so much potential. She loved and was loved." He then yanked his hand away, causing Agnar's head to drop. "But you, someone who took for granted all they had, someone who wasn't satisfied with their blessings. You threw it away all for greed and vanity."

"I'm sorry, please believe me. I knew nothing of their intent. I never wanted anyone hurt or killed. Please spare me."

Herleif could only shake his head in disappointment. "I cannot make that decision. It is up to Fate to decide."

Agnar's head snapped up, a glare on his wrinkled face. "We make our choices! What we want, we go after. There is no fate."

A chuckled escaped Herleif. "I foolishly thought the same, but I was wrong. A wise woman once told me our choices lead us to where we're supposed to be. So, Father, your choices led you to this point. You chose to lie, to let greed drive you. You have forsaken those who loved you and look where it's gotten you. Alone, angry, bitter, and withering away."

"No!" he cried once again. "Do something! I am your father! You owe me!"

"Do I?" Herleif laughed bitterly. "Shall I show the mercy you didn't? Will it somehow save Alexia? I would, for her, not you."

"Do you not care for me? Your own blood? I gave you everything!"

"You gave me grief! Blood means nothing when your actions are vile! You betrayed your blood. Your wife and your son. You are a disgrace."

Agnar tried crawling to his son but only managed to fall on his face, berating Herleif. Ignoring the man he could no longer call Father, he glanced at Alexia, now at peace.

Would she live? Her chest rose and fell with breath, but for how long?

Just as he took a step toward her, a more violent wind rent the air, so much that Herleif shielded his face with his forearm to block the debris flying around. A flash lit up the cavern and when the wind quieted, Herleif dropped his arm to stare in disbelief.

Astride an armored steed was a beautiful Valkyrie, her sky-blue eyes trained on him.

VOLUME THREE

Chapter Twelve

Alexia heard everything around her. Nonia's soft pants next to her. The shockingly sad conversation between Herleif and Agnar. The declaration of Herleif's intent to save her. The despair in his voice. She tried to speak, move, *anything*, but nothing seemed to work. She even tried to communicate through their mental link, but it was blocked.

Why? What had happened?

She remembered battling with Fenrir then calling upon everything she had, urging the souls to go through her to the afterlife. She had absorbed their power and it'd been overwhelming. Phenomenal. Empowering.

Alexia knew she wasn't dead, so why couldn't she move? Why couldn't she speak?

And who was here, leaving Herleif speechless? Neither he nor Agnar had said a word for several moments. She felt a presence—two, in fact—but couldn't distinguish who or what had joined them. She felt certain if there was a threat, Herleif would have reacted accordingly.

"Nonia, can you hear me?"

Her wolf-dog nuzzled against her side and whined then licked her cheek.

Alexia laughed to herself. *"At least you can hear me. I wish you could speak to me. And I wish I could move. I don't understand why I cannot. I need to know what's happening to Herleif."*

A beautiful, lyrical voice rang out. Another woman was in their presence.

"Your want for justice is recognized, Herleif. Tell me, what would you sacrifice in order for Alexia to survive?"

"Anything," he said immediately.

"Yourself?"

"If it were the only way."

"And if there was another way? If sacrificing your father not only brought Alexia back, but also served as justifiable punishment for his sins, what say you?"

There was silence. Alexia heard no reply from Herleif, but she suddenly felt his emotions. As much as he wanted his father to pay, he couldn't bring himself to offer him up.

"I sense your hesitation. Even now, the compassion you feel in your heart is commendable."

"It is not up to me to make that choice regarding his life, no matter how strongly I feel about the injustice he's done," Herleif said.

His father continued to remain silent, simply whimpering to himself as if he'd lost the will to even counter with more argument. No doubt he realized it was futile.

"Yet you take a life in a fight?"

"That was their choice to fight, and to fight to the death. Kill or be killed. I'll take living, thank you very much."

Sweet laughter rang out. "Such balance between brute and benevolence. It has served you well, and it will continue to serve you moving forward."

"And what of Alexia? Please tell me how to save her. I don't want to go on without her."

"And you will not have to, loyal troll."

Alexia's pulse raced. Would they have a chance at a life together? *"Herleif?"*

"Alexia?"

He heard her! Footfalls sounded off, and Nonia yipped with joy. Alexia felt Herleif near, then he caressed her cheek.

"Can you wake, my love?"

"I'm trying. Why am I having trouble moving and speaking?"

"You went through a traumatic experience," said the woman. "Your body is still processing the energy you absorbed and determining how to navigate the enormity of power without exploding."

"Oh, well, I'd rather not explode."

The woman let loose with a deep throaty laugh, so different from her speaking voice. "I promise you, that will not happen. Your strength and control are impressive."

"Thank you?"

"You're most welcome."

Alexia concentrated on that strength and control she had just been praised for. She was eager to remove herself from this almost catatonic state.

"Easy, Alexia," Herleif said. "I feel your desire to return. It will happen when ready."

"I'm ready now. Oh, I can speak again!" Herleif chuckled as she focused on movement, on opening her eyes and being able to at least sit up. When her lids opened, and her gaze connected with Herleif, she nearly cried with joy.

"Ah, there's my woman," he said.

"Here I am." Nonia yipped and sat up, waiting. "Yes, yes, I'm trying." Alexia directed her energy to her muscles, and she was able to sit. Then with the aid of Herleif, she stood. Her gaze shifted to the ethereal beauty of what could only be a Valkyrie atop a gorgeous horse.

"Oh, my! How beautiful you two are!"

The Valkyrie dipped her head, and the horse neighed. "As are you, Alexia Stavros. Now, I think it's time for you and Herleif to return to your realm while I take care of Agnar."

"What of my mother?" Herleif asked.

"She will be fine," the Valkyrie said. "Better, in fact, and you will see her soon."

"And Fenrir?" Alexia questioned. "He will no longer pose a threat?"

The Valkyrie shook her head. "His soul is bound in the depths of Hell and can never escape."

Alexia bowed her head in gratitude.

"Herleif!" his father yelled, finding his voice. "Do not let this happen! It's not my time!"

"But it is, and it is out of my hands. Your time for judgement has arrived." Alexia took Herleif's hand in hers to offer comfort, easing his grief. He gave a soft squeeze. "It's time to go," he said.

While Agnar continued to moan, the Valkyrie looked at Alexia and Herleif. "Till Valhalla, warrior and warrioress. May you enjoy a long life filled with love and purpose."

"*Takk*," Herleif said just as Alexia replied with "*Eucharist*," both thanking her.

In a flash, the Valkyrie scooped up Agnar and disappeared. Alexia felt Herleif's heart race as he took a deep breath.

"Time to return, my love," she said. And in a blink, she'd returned the two of them to her apartment while Nonia went to rest, knowing her mistress was safe. Alexia wound her arms around her troll and looked up at him. "You are an amazing being, Herleif."

"As are you." He leaned down to seal his lips to hers, kissing her gently as if she'd easily break. He broke the kiss too soon, causing her to frown.

"Herleif, I feel your hesitation. Why?"

"You've been through a lot. I'm sure you need rest." He started to pull away. "I—"

"Stop." He jerked to a halt, confusion on his

handsome face. "Don't you dare go anywhere unless it's to my bed. Or here," she pointed to the floor. "This will do just as well."

"Alexia…"

"No, do not say another word if all you're going to do is provide excuses."

"You are still processing, healing. You need rest," he stated again.

"No. I need you." To prove her point—and truthfully, to show off—she used her magic to strip them both naked and have him on his back at her feet. Surprise flashed in his eyes before desire took its place. When he started to lift his hand, reaching for her leg, she stepped away. "Lie still."

He quirked a brow but remained silent as he returned his hand to his side.

"Now, you aren't going to move, is that clear?"

"It is."

Alexia smiled as she used her foot to spread his legs apart before dropping to her knees between them. Herleif watched with what she knew was anticipation as she felt his entire body vibrate. Their bond was expanding, strengthening, and she had no doubt he could feel her excitement and desire as well.

She watched as his erection grew, its tip already moist with his cum. She hummed with delight, eager to taste him. To pleasure him. Crawling between his legs, she reached his cock, trailing a finger along its length as her other hand teased his balls. Herleif jerked and moaned, his hands clenching at his sides.

Alexia wasted no time, fisting the base of his erection while wrapping her lips around the head. His cock pulsed in her mouth as she swirled her tongue before suckling while also squeezing with her hand.

"Ahh, so good," he groaned.

She alternated between taking him deep and licking the head. Squeezing and stroking as he grew impossibly harder, his semen leaking in thick droplets along her tongue. His sounds of pleasure spurred her as she increased her actions, moving faster as she bobbed her head, taking as much of his length as she could. She felt his restraint ready to break, sensing he needed to touch her and take control. And she was ready for him to do just that.

Releasing his cock, she earned a moan of protest. "Not to worry, my handsome troll, I'm going to let you fuck me." Herleif's eyes widened causing her to laugh. "I'm learning a thing or two from you." She winked and shifted her position, turning her back to him and going onto her hands and knees. Looking over her shoulder, she wiggled her ass and received a growl in return.

In a flurry of movement, Herleif was on his knees at her backside, spreading her legs. "Are you wet and aching for me, my love?"

"I am."

"Let's see," he whispered as he held her hip with one hand while trailing the other through the crease of her ass, reaching her pussy.

Alexia lifted her rear, pressing closer to him as his fingers teased her clit. "Yes, Herleif, don't deny me."

"Never." He continued to rub her clit as he fisted his cock, tracing between her cheeks before notching it at her opening. "Hold on," he said, his voice raspy.

Without further warning, he shoved inside her, causing her to scream. But oh, it felt divine. He pulled back and slammed into her again. While teasing her clit, a hand pressed down on her back until her chest was on the floor and her ass remained in the air.

"So fucking sweet," he cooed. "This cock was meant for you."

"Yes," she moaned. "Deeper, Herleif, I want it all."

"And you shall have it."

He moved faster, drove deeper, igniting all her nerve endings. She teetered on the brink of an orgasm, her body thrumming until she thought she'd explode.

"Herleif, so close, so close. *Gods*, you feel amazing."

"I feel it, your pussy squeezing me, getting tighter," he gritted. "Come for me, Alexia. Now."

He pressed hard on her clit as he rammed into her, and her world shattered. She cried out as she met him thrust for thrust, elation infusing her body. Herleif was close, she felt it, and she wanted him to unleash his passion upon her. "Now come for me, my love," she said on shaky breaths. "Fill me with your seed."

"Yes," he groaned, pounding into her. "Take it, Alexia, take me," he said, almost pleading.

As if she wouldn't. She loved this troll, this beast, and she needed him to know the depths of her feelings. "I love you, Herleif. I want it all. All that you are."

He roared as his orgasm consumed him, pulling her into another climax as well. Together they soared, sharing this moment that would only be the beginning of more. Herleif continued to pound into her, and she took all that he gave. And when their bodies began to descend from the high, he slipped free and took them onto their sides.

"I never thought to be blessed like this," he whispered as he tightened his hold around her trembling body. "To hold someone such as you, love someone such as you, and to receive that love in return."

Alexia lifted his hand that rested across her body, kissing it. "I too, am blessed. As surly as you were (he chuckled), I fell for you, you loveable beast. And now

you are mine, my fated mate, as I am yours." She moved his hand to rest across her belly. "And she is ours."

She felt Herleif freeze, his body rigid. "She? What? How?"

Alexia chuckled. "I think you know how."

"But how can you be sure our joining has resulted in a pregnancy? And a girl?"

"I just know. She will be named Phoebe Stavros, for radiant, shining one, and she will carry on my lineage. And she won't be the only one who will bless us." She tightened her hold on his hand across her abdomen. "I will give you a son, and he will be named Bodvar. Bodvar Herleifsson." Herleif sucked in his breath, and she felt his heart race. "For warrior, another who will be just as strong and admirable as his father, fighting for all that is right in this world."

"Alexia," he murmured with such reverence in his voice. "You honor me." He kissed the back of her neck repeatedly until she rolled in his arms to face him.

"You are more than deserving, my troll. My warrior. My lover. And my mate." She kissed him fervently, pouring all her emotions of love and joy and hope into the action. "You are stuck with me."

Herleif laughed, the rich sound filling her with more happiness than she ever imagined.

"Well, if I'm going to be stuck with someone," he nipped her mouth with his teeth before kissing her in return, "I thank the gods it is you. My love. My mate. Future mother of our *barna*."

Alexia felt his cock stir, pressing into her belly, causing her to moan. Just as she lifted a leg over his hip, ready to be impaled by her beast, a jarring noise startled them both. Herleif pressed his face into her neck and groaned.

"Not again, the cock-blocker," he groused,

obviously remembering her uncle's ringtone.

Alexia let loose with howling laughter. "This time, he can wait." She raised a hand and flicked her wrist, silencing the phone. Herleif lifted his head to stare at her, and she gave him a grin. "Now, I believe you have plenty of time to fuck me. Again."

His smile was filled with wicked promises, and she looked forward to all of them being fulfilled.

The End

VOLUME THREE

EVERNIGHT PUBLISHING ®

www.evernightpublishing.com